Pastor Q and Donna
A Christmas Surprise

A Novel by

Lucy O. Heath

Author of
Rachel's Forbidden Love

The Reunion

All scripture quotations, unless otherwise indicated, are taken from the Holy Bible, King James Version KJV, (Public domain)

Names and personalities mentioned in this Novella came from characters developed in "Rachel's Forbidden Love", and "The Reunion". They are purely fictional, and in no way depict the lives of persons known, or unknown to the author.

The poems used in this book belong to the original works of the author: Lucy Heath, and may not be used, copied, or transposed in any form without prior consent of the author.
"The Christmas Story" - "The Changing of the Guard"©.

Cover design: Millennium Design Group
heathenterprise@bellsouth.net

Copyright © 2014 Lucy O. Heath
All rights reserved.

ISBN: 1499116241
ISBN 13: 9781499116243

~ Inspiration ~

I thank my Lord for the direction of the Holy Spirit Who has inspired me to write these novels. These writings are penned to reinforce the virtues I believe can still be found in true Christian romances today.

To: Sherri
No weapon formed against you...
Enjoy the READ — 3/25/17
Call me
770-987-2084

~ Dedication ~

To my son M. Quincy, who has ardently worked with me to produce these last three projects, even during the struggles of his own illness.

Prologue

September 1964

The crazy thing about unanswered questions is; the longer they go unanswered, the greater you doubt that God can answer them; and that's no frame of mind for a pastor's wife to be in.

It seems like only yesterday that I realized I was in love with Pastor Q, but it's really been more than a year ago now. He told me he knew that someday I would be his wife. He said he admired me more and more from his distant pulpit and that's when he realized he had already fallen in love with me. He claimed that no matter how hard he tried to ignore what was happening to him, his attention kept filtering back to me sitting in the fourth row of pews, on the left side of the church. That's where I sat with my mother and my daughter Lizzy. When my father was not serving his assigned Sundays as Deacon, he sat with us too.

Pastor Quincy told me that a few months after his arrival at Lighthouse Christian Ministries, he began looking forward to seeing me out in the audience, and when I wasn't there he began to notice that his enthusiasm for facing the day and delivering his sermon somehow dwindled. He was sure by then he was very much attracted to me. Quincy said it wasn't long after that, that he prayed for a way to approach me as a friend, and not as my pastor.

He also said he knew he was *lying* when he prayed that prayer. His prayers were indeed answered, but in the way the Lord saw fit for them to be answered.

He was used as my pastor to approach me with a '*Word*' from the Lord.

God established him first as a man of God who hears from the Lord and follows in obedience. Then after that, our paths kept crossing until a friendship developed.

I said '*yes*' when he proposed to me last year at Christmas time. We were at his mother's house. I was in the middle of making a very important emotional decision in my personal life at that time, and I wanted to wait until the spring of the year to set our wedding date. However, Pastor Q thought otherwise. He knew what I was getting ready to go through (concerning Lizzy), and thought it best to have someone who loved me to be at my side for support, and he was right.

We got married on Valentine's Day.

I was use to people having long engagements, you know, to get to know each other better, but I also felt the *Spirit* of the Lord merging us together.

I was prepared to be Quincy Folks' wife, but what I was not prepared for was to be the *Pastor's* wife. I had no idea of the responsibilities and issues that come with the status of being '*First Lady*'.

ONE

Now that I've spent the last hour sitting in my parent's living room, I'm beginning to feel that I've made a big mistake. I let myself in with my spare key, and found the house empty. They must have gone out to dinner to one of those buffet restaurants after service.

This wasn't the first disagreement pastor Q and I have had, but with everything else that's been going on, this one seemed to take the cake!

I was supposed to be the one he could depend on. Why did I always have to fly off the handle? Why couldn't I just swallow my pride, shut my big mouth, and listen to reason? I guess what I wanted more than anything now was for my husband to hop in his car, follow me over here, and beg me to come home. But, why should he? I didn't even give him a chance to explain anything to me.

What excuse could I give my parents for being here? I know I had a lot to learn about being a pastor's wife, but I wanted to learn them *I guess* from a book, a '<u>How To Guide For</u> <u>The Pastor's Wife</u>', not from real life experiences, or by trial and error.

Trial and error hurt too much.

Before we got married, Pastor Quincy shared with me some of the problems we might face when I became his wife. He was kind enough to say that *'we'* might face. Not every female in the congregation was going to be thrilled about our marriage. He knew that after he announced our engagement on New Year's Eve night in our *'Watch'* service, some negative encounters could begin right away.

He mentioned three women in particular who might resent him choosing me as his wife. Of course, he let me know it might not be about me personally, but just for the mere reason that he chose me instead of them. Quincy pointed out names and faces to me that week.

I knew some of the lady's casually as members, but I didn't have a *chummy* sort of relationship with them. That could have gone for most of the people at the church. I was always cordial, showing myself friendly, but between taking care of Lizzy, and working full time; I just didn't have much of a *'girlfriend' social life. Quincy promised me I had nothing to be jealous of concerning any of those women, because he never had anything socially to do with them outside of a handshake in church. In their case a* **'Holy Hug'** would be completely misunderstood.

Pastor Q and Donna

That first couple of Sundays in the New Year I began to notice happenings I had never noticed before. Maybe that's because my mind was always on the message; that is before it became obvious that some of my attention was now drawn towards the messenger.

⸺

Coming back to the present, Donna knew her eyes must have become red and puffy, so she decided to go upstairs to her old bedroom to freshen up, and maybe throw some cold water on her face. On her way up the staircase she stopped when a sudden flashback of only a year or so ago hit her. *She was almost standing in this very spot when she first realized she had fallen for Pastor Quincy Folks, and the thought of being the pastor's wife seemed appealing.*
She continued up the steps feeling a little miffed at herself for her childish reactions of the day.

Donna sat in the room that used to be hers. She had to say use to be, because it was really the extra guest room now. Well, to tell the truth, it became the guest room when she first moved out of her parent's house after she finished college.

She was twenty-one years old, on her own, and thought she could handle the world. She had a good job in corporate America, and had met a very handsome man who worked in the same building. He had not yet taken the *Bar*, but that was a breeze for him to pass. Donna had her sights on becoming his wife as soon as he was asked to become an associate.

None of that happened!

Things really got turned around when Ron invited her to a birthday party his folks were throwing for him. He had been taking her out for a while, and finally she was going to meet his parents. Needless to say, when she arrived, his parents were not expecting to see a *'girl of color'*. Evidently, they thought their son had lost his mind. They tried to be cordial, but failed miserably.

At least I had something in common with a few other folks there. Unfortunately, they were serving the champagne and hors d'oeuvres.

I should have known something was wrong. Ron didn't mind us going a few places with my friends, but we never went anywhere with his friends. Usually we dated alone, except on a few occasions when his friend Derek would happen to meet up with us at a restaurant, or a sporting event. He was always friendly, and didn't seem to mind my *color*.

That night I was so embarrassed, but basically, I was fuming mad. To think that he would put me in such an uncomfortable position knowing his family's views on interracial dating... and maybe that's why he did it in the first place. I had to get out of there, but Ron didn't want to leave his 'precious' party. He said he would call a taxi for me if I wanted to leave, but he didn't see why I was so upset. Derek saw what was going on, and volunteered to drive me home.

I should have taken the taxi.

To make a horrible story short; I ended up being forced through my apartment door, and raped by Ron's best friend. I was crying so hard and was very hysterical when I telephoned Ron. He said he didn't believe a word I said. He knew his friend, and that was the kind of lie he expected to hear coming from a girl like me... What did he mean by *'A girl like me'?* Those words hurt more than ever.

My parents took me to the emergency room. There was evidence that I was no longer a virgin, but they could not prove that I had been raped. The police questioned Ron, but he denied knowing me that well, and he told them he was only vaguely acquainted with Derek. He lied saying he had no idea of where Derek lived, or where he was.

Ron never spoke to me again, and his *friend* seemed to have vanished into thin air. I could not go in to that work place any more. It was torture. I skipped and missed several days at a time. At the point when I thought I was about to get fired, I quit. I already was behind on my rent, and Mom and Dad were praying for me to come back home. I should have known I could not have handled something of that magnitude alone without the support of my parents and the church. So, there I was jobless, broke, and pregnant. Instead of me taking the world by storm...it took me.

I thank God for my parents. They loved me unconditionally. Not only did they take me back in; but during those last seven months, they paid for me to begin going to school to get my degree in nursing. My friend Louvain Bell was the only associate I kept from the past, and she remains my friend 'till this very day.

Pastor Quincy was beside himself. How could this stupid little thing get blown out of proportion the way it did? In the half year, or so since their marriage they had many discussions about thing just like this; the fast women in the church. Its true one just can't put them out of the congregation. Some people are natural born trouble makers. The goal of the church is to reach them with the Word, so they might change, and live a righteous life.

However, after Pastor Quincy and Donna were married, some relief did come. One of the ladies left the church. Another one, feeling somewhat challenged, fancied her attentions to someone else, but Rita was not about to give up!

Quincy and Donna fasted, and prayed about the problem. He even delivered sermons about having the *'Jezebel'* spirit in the church; still the message went unheeded. He couldn't counsel Rita personally, because she would probably take it as him giving her special attention, and he wasn't about to sit in a room alone with that kind of spirit.

If Donna did the counseling, Rita would take it as Donna being jealous of her. The woman needed help. They just didn't know how to go about it at the moment.

Rita always sat two pews back from the front row, in the same seat next to the aisle. She would purposely wear low cut tops, or high-cut skirts to attract attention. When she crossed her legs, her hemline would rise even further up her thigh. As a man of God, it was always disturbing to him. This kind of behavior was not flattering. It sure wasn't enticing, at least not to him.

The church 'Mothers' tried to help by offering Rita a scarf napkin to cover herself, but she would either place it up high across her thighs, or place it over the edge of her skirt for a few minutes. Then she'd let it fall off her lap several times during the service, so she would have to lean over and pick it up. The girl needed help!

TWO

    Last week the church announced my upcoming birthday on August 17th, and those wishing to bless, or give me well wishes could do so on the Sunday before. It was my thirty-sixth birthday, still quite young (according to some) to be pastoring a congregation our size. I had been there a few years before the present growth in membership we have now took place.

    Well that's sort of how this whole mess started.

    Of course with my birthday being announced, Rita flew at the chance to buy me a birthday present. She couldn't wait; let's say...she **would** not wait to present her gift at the morning service with the rest of the congregation.

No. She somehow had to finagle her way back to my office before service started. She lied to the Amour Bearer, saying that the pastor had sent for her. When he tapped on the door to announce her, she pushed her way in. Before I could signal for him to remain in the room, she closed the door. I could feel the anger rising in my spirit, but I asked the Lord to keep me calm, while I threw her out.

Rita placed herself flat against the door and smiled. It's a good thing the door didn't lock, or I might have heard the evil *thing* 'click' it.

I stood and made my voice as dry and lifeless as possible.

"Yes *sister* Whitley. What is it? I'm really pressed for time. You know I usually don't see any parishioners before service, and I surly don't allow them to drop by unannounced."

"Yes Pastor. I know, but I knew you wouldn't mind seeing me. And, I was announced."

Quincy moved to stand beside his desk.

"Excuse me. (His voice became precise) Was there something you wanted?"

The second he heard the words leave his lips, he knew he should have phrased the sentence differently.

Pastor Q and Donna

It was too late. Rita pounced on them like *white on rice*.

"Why *yes* Pastor Q. there is, but I never thought I would hear those words coming from you."

How dare her use my wife's pet name for me.
It took all I could do to keep from walking across the room and slapping her. I had to remember I was her pastor. I put a fixed smile on my face and said:

"I think you'd better leave Sister Whitley, you don't want to be late for service."

"I just came by to say *Happy Birthday,* and to deliver my gift to you... in person."

She reached in her purse and pulled out a small gift-wrapped jewelry box. He didn't move from his desk to receive it. So, she walked across the room and placed it on the edge of the desk.

"Thank you *'Miss'* Whitley. You may leave my office, and from now on, do not show up unless you are invited."

Wherever the Amour Bearer went off to, he had returned. He gave a few light taps on the door, and opened it. I told him Sister Whitley was leaving, and I was just about to reprimand him for leaving his post, when he swung the door open even wider.

"Good morning Sister Folks", the Amour Bearer said.

Rita put a smirk on her face, and spoke with a real fake southern accent saying,

"Morning Sister Folks."

And then slithering by the Pastor's wife said,

"I just wanted to be the first one to wish your husband...I mean *my* pastor a happy birthday."

The look on Donna's face was shock, amazement, and hurt all rolled into one. You see, we had agreed that Rita was never to be alone with me in my office. Either Mrs. Daily or a church staff member was to be present.

Donna looked across the hall to Mrs. Daily's office, but she was nowhere to be seen. With a nod of my head, I told the Amour Bearer I would see him later, and allowed him to take his post at the sanctuary door.

I tried to explain to Donna what had taken place. I told her that before I knew it, Rita had maneuvered her way into the office, and she was only there for a few minutes. Donna was truly hurt because this was the private time we spent together every Sunday before I left for the pulpit. We would hold hands and pray together before I walked out to the rostrum. Now, that *witch* (excuse me Lord) ruined it. I could see that Donna was more than a little upset. When she looked at me, her beautiful eyes were filled with sadness, and disappointment. She didn't even grab my hands for prayer.

She just said her prayer was that the Lord would grant His servant strength, blessings, and peace to deliver the message he had for God's people today. Then, she turned and walked out closing the door behind her.

If it wasn't but for the grace of God, I would have torn down the hallway, flung open the sanctuary doors, and grabbed that wicked Rita around the neck and squeezed until she dropped to the floor.

I was so angry. I couldn't help it. That's what popped up in my flesh at that moment. I was about to burst, I didn't know what to do. I ran over to the desk, picked up the little box, and without so much as a glance, threw it in the wastebasket. Then, with one long sweep of my hand everything on my desk went flying to the floor.

Mrs. Daily ran across the hall, and opened the door. I had already knelt down to pick up a few of the items when she inquired if everything was all right. I nodded my head telling her yes, that I tipped something the wrong way on my desk, and everything else began to tumble over.

She probably could sense it was a little more than what I told her, and asked if I needed one of the Deacons to come in. I told her *no*, I would be just fine, and would be out in a couple of minutes.

I dropped to my other knee, and tears flooded to my eyes. My hands formed into fists pounding the floor.

"Oh Lord, have mercy on me. Forgive me for my thoughts and my actions. Take this anger away from me, and wash me clean. Help me to see the people as sheep in need of a shepherd, especially sister Rita. Give me Your eyes. Give me Your heart, and give me Your peace, in Jesus' name. Amen."

THREE

Donna sat on the edge of the bed in her old room. She knew she had done everything wrong today. She left the church as soon as the benediction was pronounced. Usually she stood with her husband to greet the congregation, or sifted through the sanctuary greeting folks on her own. But today, she left through the side doors, and went straight to the back parking lot. Donna was angry with herself, angry with her husband, and outraged at that wicked woman.

Having two cars was a blessing, but now she was not so sure how she felt about that. She was happy she didn't have to ride home with her husband, but mad at herself for taking the easy way out. What's even worse, she left her husband with the very person that instigated this whole mess. When she thought about how stupid that was of her, she got even angrier.

Donna was trying her best to be a pastor's wife, but somehow things just didn't flow like she had imagined they would. It wasn't the pastor's fault. Their love for each other was unwavering. It was this whole *'call of the ministry'* thing.

Just being a parishioner sitting in the pews every Sunday and on Wednesday nights for Bible study was certainly different from being in the leadership position she was in now. Donna knew it was a silly question to ask of God, but she asked it quite often:

> *"Why can't the ministry of **church**, flow smoothly? Why did it have to have so many hitches and turns? Where was the consistency?"* Then she would get the same, if not an almost similar answer from God every time: *"The consistency is in Me. I'm the constant, I never change."*

Donna looked at her watch. It was almost two o' clock. She thought her parents should have been home long before now. She needed some advice, and a shoulder to cry on. Maybe they had gone out to dinner after service. Come to think of it, she hadn't noticed any cook pots on the stove, or smelled any lingering orders of prepared food.

At any rate, she knew her husband should have been home by now, unless he was headed her way. Donna circled the room a few times, and then headed to the room next to it that used to belong to Lizzy. There wasn't much in it now to remind her of the precious little Amish girl she had once adopted. Her mother had turned it into a relaxation slash exercise room for herself.

She agreed with her parents that to leave it as it used to be when Lizzy was with them would only be a constant reminder of their loss too. The room now had a treadmill, some light weight bell-bars, a boom box to play cassette tapes, a small aquarium, a Chaise lounge, and a thick imitation zebra rug. It was cozy and inviting.

Donna was just about to sit on the chaise, when a noise interrupted her action. Her parents had returned. Mrs. Vaughn called up the stairs to her daughter.

"Donna, Donna. Are you upstairs?"

Donna moved across the room to the hall, and poked her head over the banister.

"Yeah, Mom."

"What on earth are you doing up there? Is Pastor Quincy with you?"

"No Mamm. It's just me. I didn't expect you and Dad to be back so soon. Did y'all go out to eat?"

Mrs. Vaughn was on her way up the stairs, but stopped half way.

"We didn't go to eat yet. We dropped Sister Richardson off, and thought we'd swing by here to change our clothes first."

I had almost forgotten that Sister Richardson was one of my folk's (and my) new undertakings. She was one of the elderly members of our church. Her husband was nearly incapacitated, and when he wasn't bed-ridden, he was in a wheelchair. Aside from the professional help that came in twice a week, she was his primary caregiver. One of the members on his side of the family, who was not a church goer, came to sit with him on Sundays while she came to service. Her husband used to be the driver of the family. She probably could have learned how to drive after he became ill, but being near seventy years old, she just didn't see the use.

By the time those few thoughts ran through my head, Mom was standing beside me at the top of the stairs.

"Okay. What is it? Something's going on young lady. You just don't *pop* in here by yourself on a Sunday afternoon; especially when you should be with your husband."

Before I could answer, Mom yelled down the stairs to Dad saying she would be down in a few minutes. She turned and headed down the hall towards her bedroom, and without even looking back said;

"Follow me."

I began to tell her all that had happened this morning, and although she was a little surprised, she was not shocked. Mom said she was wondering when *"Miss Thing"* was going to make her move, and when she did; she hoped I would be ready for it. Looks like I wasn't. I was too upset, and embarrassed to go home, so I asked her if I could spend the night there.

"What!"

The level of her voice jumped two octaves. Anyone would have thought I had just asked her to commit a mortal sin.

"Look Donna, I love you very much, and I love Pastor Quincy too. There are certain things in marriage that you have to figure out for yourself, and it's not for me to put any suggestions in your head. Although, I do believe I've... we've raise you to be a responsible adult.

This house has been a peaceful haven for many people, including you in a time of need, but it's not a hideout.

You get answers to problems in marriage by coming together to work them out, not by running away and avoiding them. So, my motherly advice to you is to pray about what God is saying for you to do. Take as long as you want. Hear God good… only don't be here when your father and I get back from dinner."

Mrs. Vaughn patted Donna on the knee, and got up from where she was sitting to put her heels in the closet. She grabbed a pair of flats, slipped her feet into them, and went to the bedroom door. She looked back over her shoulder, and gave a loving smile to her daughter who was still sitting on the bed.

"Don't worry honey. Everything will work out all right. If you let this *'mole hill'* become a mountain, what will you do when the hard tests come along?"

She walked down the hallway. A few seconds later Donna heard the front door click, and she was left alone to hear from the Lord for herself.

FOUR

Pastor Folk's fury had subsided to a mere disappointment. His concern now was for his wife. He knew her well enough to know that she ended up at her parent's house, but wasn't sure how much she would share with them concerning this morning. His Father and Mother-in-law were good solid Christians, and he was confident that whatever advice they gave their daughter would be without prejudice. Quincy had wanted more than anything to tear out of the back doors of the church as soon as service was over. He wanted to follow Donna, but he was still receiving birthday wishes from the parishioners; and making light excuses for his wife's absence. His biggest problem was trying to avoid Rita.

He felt strongly about going over to the Vaughn's, but a little small voice in his head said: *'go home'*. He knew that was the right thing to do, because he needed to pray and think things through too. No good could come of anything if both of them were upset, especially in front of her parents. Three things ran through his mind. He knew she was new at being a pastor's wife', he was their son-in-law, and he was their pastor. In the role of pastor, he must allow wisdom to dictate temperance, and maturity.

Several unpleasant things had come up against his wife since their marriage, but what Donna did not seem to understand is these things weren't necessarily about her. They were formed against her by the enemy! That's the way he works. He comes up against the things of God. His mission is to steal, kill, and to destroy. If he can break up a marriage, (especially a pastor's) he could probably tear down the congregation and break up the church. That's his objective. *Oh, not just the church I pastor,* Quincy thought, *but The Church of God.* Well, he's not going to sneak in and destroy what I love. Quincy was talking out loud. "And, that goes for my wife, and the church!"

One of the things he heard from the Lord was to stand still. As much as he wanted to, he couldn't run after Donna every time she ran away from her problems. If he did, she would never learn how to walk in her own strength. Yes, he is her pastor, and her husband, but she needed to develop greater faith for the position that had come to her through marriage. She has to get a deeper sense of, *'you can't be joined to the man without being joined to his mantle'*.

Quincy sat for a while longer decreeing and declaring the blessings of Abraham on their lives. He felt a little tinge of hunger, and remembered he had only eaten some fresh fruit, a slice of cheddar cheese, and drank a half-cup of ginger tea before leaving the house this morning. As hungry as he was, he still couldn't bring himself to move from the chair he'd plopped in when he hit the front door.

He looked around the nicely decorated living room. It was an OK room before; but now, since he's been married, Donna's finishing touches did even more to improve its appearances. It was even more warm and inviting than it used to be. Everything she did was nice. She had a way of making everything seem beautiful. She had the ability to enhance without changing who he was. *'If that makes any sense'*, he thought. He thought the thought through, and speaking out loud again said, "Yes, that does make sense, because that's what marriage is! Enhancing the other person, but without changing who God designed them to be".

"I totally agree."

Donna was leaning on the slender petition wall between the open serving window in the kitchen, and the entrance to the living room. Quincy looked up having a befuddled expression on his face. During his musing, he had not heard his wife come in.

"Is that as far as you got?" Donna said, laying her purse and keys on the counter.

"Yah, I guess I'm a little more fatigued than I thought."

Donna's heart was melting, but she didn't dare move from where she was standing. She needed to apologize to her husband for acting in such an immature way this morning. She allowed the enemy to walk right in and use her. Donna knew her husband well enough to know that what happened this morning was not his fault. She played right into the hands of the adversary, and hated herself for being that weak and gullible.

While sitting at her parent's house, she realized that she permitted herself to be cheated out of her role as *'help mate'*. Throughout the entire service she was so puffed with anger, she had no idea what the sermon was about. What's more, she abandoned her husband leaving him without the faithful covering of prayer and the 'Word' over him during the service.

When she looked up, her husband had pulled himself up from where he was seated in the chair. Donna wasn't sure if he would walk towards her, or if he would walk towards the stairs. She quickly took the few steps across the open living room to stand in front of him.

"Quincy, I'm sorry. I apologize for my actions today, but most of all, I apologize for letting you down as a wife."

Tears were already spelling over her bottom lashes, and she could feel that she would soon be in need of some tissue for her nose. Quincy moved in to embrace his wife. He put both arms around her waist. He kissed her on the forehead, and was on a direct path to her lips when she pulled back.

"What's wrong?"

"Quincy, my face is a mess. Besides, we have to talk."

Pastor Folks reached in the back right pocket of his pants, and pulled out a handkerchief. He gave it to his wife, still holding his embrace on her with his left hand. Donna dabbed at the trickling tears and her almost leaky nose. Her husband smiled to himself as the thought ran through his mind of the many times he aided his wife with a handkerchief. More of his handkerchiefs were soiled with her makeup and tears, than with his own sweat. All of a sudden his stomach rumbled with the reminder of hunger. Then Donna suggested they go out to dinner, and they could finish their talk.

"Well, why can't we talk right here? We can get something out of the fridge."

He moved in to draw his wife against him.

"Because, one; I don't want to be preparing food while we are talking, and two; I want to sit across the table from you and share what's on my heart."

Pastor Folks put his right arm back around her waist.

"Gee honey, can't we stay right here and do that?"

She was almost swayed by her husband's magnetic hold. It wasn't what he said; *it was the way he said it.*

"No", she managed to say. "That's just what I'm talking about."

Donna wiggled to release his embrace.

"I'm serious Quincy."

He lowered his voice to a husky baritone sound, and said,

"So am I."

Donna broke his hold, and stepped back.

"Look, I know you've already forgiven me. But, I just can't move away from this as easily as you can. What I mean is that you're more experienced in dealing with these kinds of situations than I am, and I need to talk things through."

Quincy raised his left eyebrow causing a wrinkle to form across his forehead.

"Wait a minute! I'm *more* experienced in dealing with what *kind* of situation?"

"O boy. I guess that didn't come out right. What I meant was, that you told me of a few women in the congregation who didn't mind letting you know…well, about their interest in you, and in a way you've always been the *rejecter,* instead of the *rejectee.*"

"I guess I'm not quite following you."

Tears started to well up in Donna's eyes once more. Through sniffles she said,

"I feel like in every event in my life, I have been the rejected one."

"I hope not in *every* event", Quincy said, trying to brush her lips.

Donna stopped her sniffling.

"Oh Q, I didn't mean *every* event. Marrying you was the best thing that ever happened to me. Outside of salvation and the Lord, I love you more than anything."

She looked up into her husband's face. Quincy reached to embrace her again, and she let him.

"And you are the love of my life too. I love you more than anything."

Now, Donna's eyebrow arched a little. It wasn't what he said, but the way he said it. She took a step back, and took a deeper look at her husband's expression. She gave him a playful punch on the shoulder.

"You see; that's what I'm talking about. In the few short minutes we've been talking, your mind has gone from your stomach, to the bedroom, to hearing little of what I said; because it moved back to the bedroom again. That's why we have to get out of the house to have this talk."

Donna tried to act peeved, but she really wasn't.

"Okay, okay. I surrender. We'll go out and talk, but just to let you know one thing Mrs. Donna *—smarty-pants* Folks, My mind never left the bedroom!"

He grabbed his suit jacket from the chair, and they left through the front door.

FIVE

The dinner meeting went well for Pastor Quincy and Donna. He understood better what seemed to be bothering his wife. It was more than the immediate problem.

Maybe they still needed to search out a Christian counselor after all.

Some of the things she was feeling came from unhealed wombs in her past. The best thing he could do as her husband was to keep showing her how much he loved her, and to keep praying over her.

One of the things he wanted to encourage her in was to become more involved in the ministry. Although she was there every Sunday, and most Wednesday evenings, he was pretty sure if she became active in a hands-on way, she would feel more useful and needed. Donna was intelligent. She was a nurse, and only in her mid-twenties, (*not that far removed from the youth in the church*). Maybe teaching one of the Sunday school classes, or developing one of her own would help to inspire her.

Before they left the restaurant they came up with an idea on how to handle the *"Rita"* situation.

They needed something clever, but not devious; something that would show they were unified as a couple, but wouldn't come off as Donna being jealous of '*Miss Thing*'. First they had to go back to the church to get whatever it was that Rita had given him for a gift. Quincy had no idea what it was. He told Donna he was so angry, he threw it in the wastebasket, unopened.

They drove to the church, and parked the car at the back door. Quincy unlocked the door, and flicked on the switch for the hallway lights. Donna couldn't help but think that only a few hours ago she came down this very hallway headed out the door in a much different frame of mind. Her heart, at this time was so full of love for her husband she wanted to reach for his hand and give it a tender squeeze, but she didn't. She was not certain if the feelings that rose up in him while he was home had dwindled, so she didn't want to do anything to re-ignite the moment before they got back to the house.

Pastor Q and Donna

Pastor Q turned on the lights, and gave the office a quick scan to make sure everything was back in place from this morning's flair up. The church custodian came in on Mondays, and Fridays to clean, so he knew the wastebasket had not been emptied yet. He went to the trash and retrieved the article. It felt like a slight surge of anger wanted to return, but he denounced it. He handed the box to his wife, and sat on the edge of the desk. He didn't say anything, but shook his head back and forth. He must have had an expression on his face of pure discuss, because Donna said,

"Now... Quincy. There's no use getting upset all over again about this. We've already come up with what we're going to do."

Before she could say another word, He hopped up from the desk. His hands had formed into two fists, and his teeth were clenched. He walked over to the window, and she heard a noise coming from his throat that sounded like a cross between a groan and a lion's growl.

Donna kept her silence.
She knew what was happening.

A man had to have a way to vent...to let off steam.
He was cheated out of that this morning, because he had to go out and minister to the people. Quincy had to stifle any pent up actions, and move on with what the Lord had for him to do. Remembering how she was no

encouragement to him at all this morning sent a wave of guilt over her spirit. She felt awful for the cold hard stare she kept on her face during service.

How could she have been so selfish, and acted so childish?

She had her opportunity to vent, to work through her anger and frustration, why deny him his?

When her husband seemed to have calmed down, Donna went to him and placed her hand on his shoulder.

She apologized again.

She still was careful to stand her distance, because *now*, she was feeling drawn to him. She knew how easy he was to forgive when a certain intimacy had entered his mind, and if she was honest with herself, it was on her mind too.

Back to the task at hand, Donna unwrapped the package, and removed the top. They viewed the contents, and knew it would work perfectly for what they had planned.

During their dinner, Donna expressed many things, and Quincy expressed one of his own; not about her personal problem, but about their unity as a couple. It wasn't that they were not united in their marriage; he just thought a stronger unified front would be more beneficial to the ministry. Starting this coming Sunday, he wanted Donna to sit on the platform with him. It not only would present them as united in the ministry, but it would also give his wife a chance to see what he saw every week... the people!

They always prayed together for the congregation, and he believed their prayers could reach another level when the watchful eye of his helpmate was on cue. Some things a pastor prayed for concerning the flock came from the *Spirit,* other things you prayed for because you could physically see it in their faces, or in their actions. One's discernment could sense the story behind the window of their eyes, and the silence of their lips.

This Sunday Donna was to sit where she usually sat, and he would call her to the podium at some point during the service.

The gold cross in the box was perfect, not too big, and not too small. Donna decided she would take it to a jeweler and have it engraved. She would use the same paper and ribbon to rewrap the gift, so it would be ready for next Sunday.

With that decided and done, Quincy said he would get the office lights, so Donna headed for the door. Before she opened the door her husband come to stand directly behind her. She felt his hand on the small of her back, and the other one came up to rest on the closed door. His position caused his body to lean into hers, and she could feel his breath on the back of her neck. Donna drew in a deep breath, and tried to speak calmly because she knew where this could lead.

"Pastor Folks."

She felt a slight press of his lips on the back of her neck. She dare not move, or turn to face him so, she talked into the door. Feeling the blood rush through her veins, she steadied her voice:

"Pastor Folks. Do you remember our promise to each other, and your promise to the Lord (her voice quivered a little); that when you are in this office; it is holy ground and dedicated to God."

He didn't respond. Donna cleared her throat, and tried to sound sterner.

"Pastor Q, didn't you say the first day you summoned me to this office, the Holy Spirit reminded you to stay focused on *His* agenda in this workplace, and not *your* own?"

She felt, *more so than heard* a whoosh of breath on the back of her neck, and his hand slowly dropped from the door. Her body remained still, but her knees began to shake. At that moment she wanted this man of God to have his way more than ever, and it took everything within her to resist his intended advances.

Dragging his words out one by one, he said,

"M-a-n-n! Why- did- you- have- to- remember- *that* - at –a- time- like- *this*?"

"Because", Donna said. "You just elevated me to be a better helpmate for you, and this seemed to be the perfect time to start."

Quincy gave a strained laugh, and said between drawn lips.

"You got the assignment right, but your timing is a tad off."

"Oh no it's not!"

Donna turned the doorknob, and walked into the hall.

When they were headed down the highway on the way home, she kicked her heels off, and wiggled her toes. Next, she reached up and undid the garter strap from one of her stockings. Turning slightly and looking out of the corner of his eye Quincy asked,

"What in the world do you think you are doing?"

She didn't answer, but flashed a quirky smile at her husband, and took the bobby pins out of her up-do, to let her hair fall down around her shoulders. Donna began to peel one of the stockings off her shapely, smooth leg. Then giving her husband another girlish under eyed look said,

> "In your office I did my duty as your *partner* in ministry. Now, as your wife, I'm trying to *redeem the times* before we get home."

Pastor Quincy felt the excitement of the office encounter resurfacing.

> "Look here young lady. Don't make me have to stop, and pull this car over!"

SIX

Donna had made a few turns after she picked up Sister Richardson, and as strange as it seemed, it appeared that she was being followed. Looking in her rearview mirror, she noticed the car behind her going in her direction. She began to become a little antsy, but did not want to alarm Mother Richardson. Their upcoming stop was at the grocery store. It was always the last stop of her errands with the elderly woman, because of purchasing items that would need to be refrigerated within the next half hour, or so.

She still had the eerie feeling that someone was following her when she parked at the grocery store.

There were so many shoppers in the store, and Donna wasn't even sure that the suspected follower had come in to the market. She whispered a prayer while helping the elderly lady do her shopping. She prayed against the spirit of fear. Donna picked up a few items for herself and placed them in the top section of the buggy, then made her way to the checkout counter. She gave a friendly smile to people who looked her way, but she didn't recognize any of their faces anyway. After all, this wasn't her usual place to get groceries.

She and Pastor Quincy did their shopping closer to where they lived. Just the thought of her husband's name floating across her mind brought a smile to her face, as she thought about…yesterday afternoon.

When she came to herself, she was next in line. A wave of embarrassment flushed over her face. She was hoping she didn't hold up anyone in line. Well, maybe she didn't because no one had to call her name, or say… *lady, you're next!*

Donna was glad she didn't have to rush off to work today. This was one of the Mondays she took off during the month. Now that she was married, she tried to un-schedule herself at least once, or twice a month on Mondays. The other Mondays she worked second shift. These changes gave her *a relaxed down day* with her husband, because as ministry goes; some Sundays were longer, or more intense than others. So, Mondays were well deserved *'Me'* days for her husband, and she wanted to be available to make sure he got the peace and refreshing he needed.

When Donna got home, she told her husband about the feelings she experienced. They couldn't think of why anyone would be following her around town. They laughed together saying that if it were he being followed, it probably would have been Rita, but thank God she had a job to go to, and she loved money too much to miss a day's work.

They agreed in prayer asking God to reveal, and to expose whoever it was, and not to let this loom over Donna for any length of time. Quincy prayed for her protection, and asked God to set a guard of angels about her.

The next few days went well, and they even talked about going to Wilmington, Delaware the last week of the month for *'August Courtly'*. It had been a while since they visited with Mrs. Folks, and Donna really wanted to sit with her mother-in-law, and glean from her good advice, and her 'First Lady' experience. There were just too many issues popping up, and an experienced voice would be welcomed.

When Sunday morning rolled around, Pastor Quincy and Donna were very much at peace with the Lord, and were confident that they had come up with the correct way to handle the *'Rita'* problem.

They prayed together in his office, and then Donna went to the sanctuary to take her usual seat on the front pew. After the announcements the clerk turned the service back into the hands of the pastor for pulpit announcements and remarks. Pastor Folks began by thanking the entire congregation for their thoughtfulness on remembering his birthday. He then asked his wife to join him so they could make a special presentation. Pastor Folks stepped down from the stage, and took Donna's hand.

"Brothers and Sisters, I am humbled and pleased for the special care and attention you give to the *'First Lady'* and to me, and one of the things we hope to do more of in the future, is to show how much we appreciate you.

So, this morning we would like to begin with one who has been a blessing to the ministry, and not just to me, but I believe to all of us here in some way or the other. Sister Daily, will you please step forward?"

The congregation started applauding, and some of the people stood. You could hear Amen coming from others.

"Sister Daily, thank you so much for all you do around Lighthouse Ministries. We know that keeping up with as much as you do is not an easy task. Especially since the ministry has grown over the past few years. Yet, you haven't complained about it, at least not in front of me."

Pastor Q and Donna

He tilted his head, and shot his eyes in her direction. That brought a round of chuckles from the audience.

"You volunteer your services, and work as if you were getting paid. For that reason, my wife and I say thank you."

Donna took an envelope from behind her back and gave it to Mrs. Daily, and said:

"We could never pay you for all you do, but this is a card and a little something to say thank you."

Pastor Folks slipped his hand in his suit jacket pocket and pulled out a small box wrapped in pretty paper. It had a nice hand tied bow on it. He presented it to her, and said it was from the both of them. Mrs. Daily thanked them again, as well as thanking the members. Everyone stood and applauded again; except for one member who recognized the small wrapped package, and remained seated.

Mrs. Daily returned to her seat, and searched for the handkerchief in her purse. When everyone was seated, Pastor Folks spoke again.

"Speaking of appreciating people, I'd like to say how much I appreciate this *f i n e* looking young lady standing here beside me."

There were some *ooh's*, and Amen' escaping from the assembly.

"And, because she has been a true helpmate in my life; from this Sunday on, my wife will be sitting on the roster with me."

A few said 'amen', 'it's about time', and others said 'go head Pastor Folk's'. A few said nothing at all.

Pastor Folks waited at the bottom of the landing until Donna went to collect her things from her previous seat on the front row.

A certain parishioner got up and walked out of the church. Quincy Folks locked arms with his wife as they ascended the pulpit steps. When it was time for the message, he got up, gave his wife a quick kiss on the cheek… and preached like a crazy man!

SEVEN

This was one of the Mondays Donna went in to work. It meant getting up early and leaving her husband in bed.

When they were first married, she wanted to fix breakfast for him every morning before she left out for work, but he told her that wouldn't be necessary. Besides, he was hoping she would cut back on even more of her work hours. He loved his growing congregation. He knew what the financial budget was, and still they agreed to give him a raise in salary after he married Donna. It wasn't a great sum, but it showed how much they appreciated their pastor.

He also reminded his wife that he was a bachelor for many years before he married her, and as unflattering as it was for him to admit, he knew his way around a kitchen quite well. Donna couldn't argue with him on that point. As a matter of fact, she rather enjoyed coming home, every now and then to a dinner all prepared and waiting for her.

They shared equally in that particular household responsibility. They jokingly agreed to keep it a family secret. One, because he didn't want to put unnecessary pressure on the other husbands in the congregation, and two, because they could almost sense the tongue wagging it would stir if the ladies of the church thought Sister Folks wasn't taking good care of their pastor saying, *"ain't it a shame. He married that pretty young thing, and she can't cook a lick!"*

Of course they would have forgotten that only less than a year ago, she lived with her parents, and she had a three-year old child to take care of. Lighthouse Christian Ministries was her church before she married the pastor, and she knew the devil would use any tactic he could to bring a wedge between God's church and *His* appointed shepherd.

Donna had completely forgotten about last Monday's incident, until it appeared like the vehicle behind her was indeed following her. She was almost at the hospital. Maybe she was just imaging things, because looking in the rear view mirror; the vehicle now seemed to be lagging behind in the other lane beside her. Donna drove up the slop. She pulled up to the employee parking lot gate losing sight of the vehicle. She took her pass card from behind the sun visor.

What if that car turned in the visitor parking lot?

She inserted her card in the slot, and the automatic arm rose up to let her car enter. She quoted 2 Tim. 1:7 again and also asked God to expose whomever it was that was following her. She was sure of it now. If there was one thing she despised…it was a sneaking coward.

Donna was going to give her husband a call, but decided against it. She knew the more you dwell on a thing, especially the negative, the more prevalent it becomes. The morning was moderately busy, so Donna worked through her usual mid-morning break time. The growl in her stomach reminded her that it was not a good idea to skip lunch. She took the elevator one floor up to walk to the hospital cafeteria. Donna knew grabbing a tray and going through the line for some real food was what she needed to do, but she opted out for the vending machine…again. For some reason, today, she just felt like having some alone time, not mixing with other staff.

She told herself a week or so ago she needed to prepare more home-cooked meals so she could at least have decent leftovers to make for lunch the next day. It was healthier, and would probably save a little money too. All this vending snacking was putting on a little more weight than she desired.

Of course, less than a year ago she was a more active person chasing around after a three-year old. Donna was still trying to work through her empty nest syndrome. She kept her counseling sessions with the psychologist at the clinic, but couldn't get use to these unexpected setbacks that triggered her grief. This must have been one of those days.

Donna had almost reached her office when the receptionist at the nurse's station flagged her down. She was waving a small envelope in the air. Donna rearranged her parcels, and took the envelope from her hand. The envelope was about the size of a *'Thank You'* note, or an invitation to something. It was addressed to **Donna Vaughn-Folks**. *That's strange,* she thought, *I don't hyphenate my name. Since I married Quincy, I only use his last name.* She must have had a puzzling look on her face, because the receptionist hunched her shoulders in the air and said,

> "Don't ask me. I asked the gentleman if he wanted me to page you to your office, but he said no, he couldn't wait; to just see that you got the note."

Then she added,

> "And, I must say, he was pretty darn good looking for a...*non* brother."

Donna rolled her eyes in the air to the girl behind the desk, and thought, *every man is good looking to her; if he's alive and breathing!*

She entered the office, and sat her things down on her desk. Donna opened the small envelope. It was one of those cards that was blank on the inside, so you could write you own message. There was no name, or signature in the card, only the words: **CALL ME ON MATTER OF IMPORTANCE**, and a phone number.

What in the world? Her mind went immediately to whoever must have been following her. She thought; *what kind of coward would leave a note like this for a married woman? He must be crazy.*

"Hey, what if he is crazy?"

He could have some kind of mental problem. Nah, that can't be true; after all, he has enough sense to follow me around. He had enough sense to write this note, and deliver it to my workplace. Then she thought out loud again.

"That only proves that he's not retarded. He still could be some kind of a nut!"

Donna called Quincy to say she was leaving work early. She tried to speak as calmly as she could, but he must have picked up on something in her voice anyway. She told him not to worry, that she would explain everything when she got home. Pastor Q put away the remainder of the fixings he had prepared for his lunch, and put some water in the teapot. He put the saucer he used for his sandwich in the sink along with his empty drink glass.

Next, he wet the dishcloth, and wiped the scattered crumbs from the counter, and checked to see how the floor was looking.

It was okay.

Not knowing what to expect, he prayed for the blood of Jesus to cover them in their time of need, and that as a *provider-protector*, he would have the power and wisdom to meet whatever need had arisen. She didn't say that it was an emergency, or that it had anything to do with family. He didn't know what it was. He had hoped the Rita thing was settled.

EIGHT

This was certainly unexpected. Quincy thought it might have been something that had arisen again concerning Rita. Donna did mention to him the strange feelings she had about being followed, but now, what could have been taken as coincidental, was indeed a reality. They prayed an aggressive prayer of faith, thanking God for His providential care and protection. They prayed John 14:13,14 that if any evil spirit was following Donna, the Lord would force and drive it into the Abyss, along with any replacements, or assignments that was set against their family, their property, home and work place.

Pastor Q said they should go on a fast together. He took the note and placed it in his Bible until he heard from the Lord as to what he should do about it. They agreed that Donna should still go into work, that is, if she felt comfortable about it.

She said she wasn't going to let the enemy intimidate her. She admitted to having the spirit of fear concerning some things, but cowering to the devil was not one of them.

They would begin the fast right away. They would drink a hot herbal tea that night, and continue to read the Word for strength. Although Donna really needed the loving comfort of her husband's arms, they agreed to abstain from physical intimacy as part of their fast. The increased time of reading scriptures, having praise and devotion together, along with prayer and meditation would hopefully carry them beyond the longings of the flesh.

The next morning Donna went to work encouraged in the Spirit. Quincy agreed to come and share the lunch hour with her. It would help both of them strengthen themselves against the temptation of eating.

Donna suggested they meet in the park across the street from the hospital. Quincy was going to be ready with more scriptures for them to read, and would bring a thermos of special ginger tea with fresh ground cinnamon.

Since she had to be to work at seven in the morning; her lunch was scheduled for eleven o'clock. It was nearing the end of August, and the weather was hot and sunny. Maybe she should have asked her husband to fix some iced tea instead. *Nah,* ginger tea with cinnamon taste better hot than cold. The day went by surprisingly fast, and before she knew it, she was on her way out the building and across the street to meet her husband.

The traffic light changed and caught her at the curb. She took the moment to draw in a couple of deep breaths, and to enjoy the sun beaming down on her head. The hospital kept its temperature a little on the cool side, and it was nice to feel the warmth of the sun.

Donna looked up at the sky, and when she looked back down to see if the light had changed, her eyes did a slight jolt. She thought the Caucasian man in the car two lanes over looked somewhat familiar. The traffic was slow moving through the intersection, but cars were still trying to make the light before it turned red. She felt a squeamish twirl in her stomach, and her breath caught in her throat. She blew out her breath in a couple of short pants, and shook her head to clear it.

"Nah, it couldn't be." Donna spoke out loud.

By then the light had turned green, and those who stood with her on the curb began to mingle across the street. Donna ran to the center of the lane trying to get a better look at the vehicle and its passenger, but it was already too far past the intersection.

She walked down the path to where she and Quincy were supposed to meet. Her brain was still trying to process the image of the man in the car. She had only a glimpse, but she knew she had seen that face before. Who was he? Quincy rose from the bench when he saw Donna coming his way. She was a beautiful woman. *I'm a very blessed guy;* he thought. He gave his wife a light embrace, and immediately sensed the strained look on her face. They sat down, and Donna explained what just occurred at the light. She said she could not be sure, but maybe it was the same car she saw last week. It was the person driving the car she never got a chance to see. Quincy's anger surfaced again.

"How dare some cowardly idiot stalk my wife"!

He probably should not have voiced that out loud; but he was her protector, her covering, and this *clown* was getting on his nerves.
 He could see Donna was becoming more uneasy. Quincy suggested for her to take the rest of the day off, but she assured him that she would be all right. Still, he wanted to walk her back to the building, and see her safely to her office.

      ⌒⌒

 Donna knew the afternoon would be light. They rarely scheduled a patient for radiology after the noon hour. Her lunch was from 11:00p to 12:00p and her shift ended at 2:30p. The attendant at the nurse's station greeted Donna and her husband. There was no late scheduling, so all she had to do was log the day's activities in the computer, and see that the department was staffed for the evening. The last thing was to double check all the equipment and machines, and she would be done for the day. Pastor Q walked Donna the short distance from the nurses' station to her door where he planned to give her a nice peck on the cheek, and let her finish her work.

Donna pushed the door open, and Quincy walked in behind her. He stepped on something lying on the floor. He reached down to pick up a small envelope similar to the one his wife had previously received. It was addressed with only the first name...<u>Donna.</u> Quincy quickly swung the door back open, and looked up and down the corridor. Turning back to the room, Donna was already headed for the chair at her desk. He told her to sit for a moment, and not to worry about anything. He would be back in a minute. He hurtled the corridor in about three bounds.

...So far as she knew, the nurse said, no one had inquired after Mrs. Folks today, or had gone to her office. She did say someone could have gone unnoticed when she was checking files on the other side of the enclosed nurses' station.

Pastor Q stood a few feet from the desk and opened the note. He read it silently. <u>Where is Lizzy?</u> He froze in his tracks.

"What the Devil"??? *'What kind of uncircumcised Philistine would write a note like this?'*

He knew it must have been the Lord Who prompted him to walk his wife back to her office. What if she had found the note? Quincy hated to think of the trauma it would have caused her. It had only been nine months since Lizzy was back with her natural parents, and though she kept it very well masked; Donna was still working through her grief. He put the note in his pocket, and prayed for the best way to handle this whole ordeal.

What kind of an idiot would do a thing like this?

The look on Donna's face was intense, but it didn't necessarily show fear. Before she could say anything, Quincy spoke up.

"I read the note, and yes, it looks like it is from the same person."

He was careful not to say, 'nut', or imbecile.

"Who knows", he continued, laughing nervously. "Maybe you have a secret admirer or something."

Donna relaxed a little, but her eyes were searching her husband's face.

"That's not funny Q. Well, what did the note say"?

Her question caught him off guard. Quincy had to think fast.

"O, just a word or two of greeting. However my lovely lady, if this note is a partner to the first one that had a number on it, I do believe he will be getting a phone call from your illustrious husband."

"Quincy, do you think I'm in any danger? I mean, this isn't some kind of Kook, or somebody like that, is it?"

"Nah, I don't believe there's any danger, but if it will make you feel better, why don't you see if you can leave early today?"

"Well, I do have everything from today's procedures logged in the computer already, and I could complete the rest of what I have to do in the next half hour, or so. I'll go check with my supervisor."

Quincy looked at his wife, and gave her a confident smile.

"Sounds like a plan to me. I'll just wait here in your office, we can go home together."

"But Q, both of us have our cars."

"That's okay, I can follow you."

He moved in for the kiss he never got from his wife when they first came to her office. He kissed her, and lingered a moment. He forgot it was supposed to be a quick peck on the cheek.

"Besides", he said, "I don't mind following behind such a fine... *fine* (his hands were inching down below her waist).

Donna stepped back, and gave him a...

"QUINCY", in her lecturing voice!

Throwing both hands up in the air, as if he was under arrest, he said:

"What? What's wrong? All I was going to say is I don't mind following you home in your *fine* looking car."

"You ought to be ashamed of yourself. That was the *worst* lying I have ever heard. But what else should I expect from a true man of God? You can't even lie good."

He didn't want to get in the habit of lying, but he hoped she didn't see through the one he just told about the note.

NINE

Pastor Folks knew he couldn't lay aside his ministerial calling for his personal feelings. He understood the call was always with him and *in* him, no matter what.

He also understood that he was a man. He was a husband who loved his wife, and he'd be dogged gone if this fool thought that he was going to stand by and do nothing, just because he was a man of the cloth.

There are some feelings he just refused to stifle!

He knew his spirit was disturb, so just in case things didn't go so well when he met with the person, whoever he was; he made a phone call to Deacon Peters last night, and asked him to teach the Wednesday night Bible study meeting. He told him he could continue on the lesson they had been studying, or he could choose something else.

It wasn't that Pastor Folks had plans to harbor ill feeling in his heart; but if he didn't come out of this encounter untainted, he knew better than to minister God's word through a bruised spirit.

Quincy didn't often keep things from his wife, but he thought it best she not know his plans for today. After he met with whoever this joker was, depending on the outcome; he would then decide if to let her know what it was all about.

Yesterday when they got home, Donna went upstairs to relax in a soothing bubble bath, and while she was doing that, he took the first note out from his Bible, and made a phone call. The number was not to a residence, but to an attorney's office. He thought that was odd. *Why would an attorney follow someone around town, or leave notes at their work place?*

The voice on the other end of the line answered by saying; "Roberts, Roberts, and Baker, how may I direct your call?" He told the receptionist he did not have an appointment, and he was not sure who could help him. He worded his request in a way that sounded like he was asked to call this number personally. He gave her the name Vaughn, and she asked him to hold the line for a minute. A few seconds later a voice on the other end said,

Pastor Q and Donna

"Hello, this is Ron Baker."

Quincy didn't mean to sound so abrupt, but it just slipped out.
"Yes. This is Pastor Quincy Folks, and if you don't mind, you can tell me why you're following my *wife* around town, and leaving notes on her job!"

Evidently expecting to hear from Donna, but hearing her husband's voice instead; startled the man and threw him off guard.

"Oh, Mister Fol...Folks, I..."

"Look". Quincy said, "I don't know who you are, or what you're trying to pull, but this is the last note you're going to write to my wife. And, just so you will know, she didn't get the one you left under her office door today. I intercepted it!"

"Mister Folks, sir, I'm sorry. I guess I went about this in the wrong way."

Quincy could feel his temper rising.

"You're da..."

He almost reached back and grabbed a cuss word from the past, but forced out,

"You're darn straight!" (Remembering he had introduced himself as Pastor Folks)

"I apologize again sir, but if you could meet with me at my office, let's say tomorrow morning, I can assure you that I will explain everything to your understanding."

Quincy didn't like it, but he agreed. He paced the floor several times before going upstairs to see how Donna was coming along. He still hadn't settled down, and he didn't want Donna to see him like this. She would probably sense that something was wrong, so he tapped on the bathroom door to tell her that he was leaving to get Chinese take-out for dinner. He knew the drive would do him good.

Quincy took the long way around. He had to think.

Boy, I almost blew it.
Man that gives me something to think about. If I had let myself slip with that one little word; I could feel a whole string of other swear words jumping into play and ready to be used. Wow! What's so funny about it is I never used some of those words before I got saved, let alone having them come up in me after salvation. Why is the Devil so anxious to see Christians fall?
I guess that's a silly question to ask. He hates God, and he hates people who love God. He hates anyone who claims the name of Jesus, and he hates pastors even more!

Pastor Q and Donna

Quincy placed his order, adding in two extra egg rolls. The ride back to the house was a little more relaxing. For right now, he had to put tomorrow out of his mind, and concentrate on something that brought joy to his heart and a smile to his face...Donna.

―――

As the elevator rose to the fifth floor of the Park Office Building, Pastor Folks kept praying in order to keep his temper from doing the same thing the elevator was doing... rising!

It wasn't until this morning that the Holy Spirit revealed to him who Ron was. He never connected the name with the old boyfriend. When it came to him, he was livid. He was also relieved it didn't dawn on him yesterday. If it had, he probably would have headed straight over here instead of going to get Chinese food.

He did not have to wait. The door marked *'private'* opened as soon as he was announced. The man, about thirty-fiveish or so, gave orders to the secretary not to be disturbed, and to hold all phone calls. The young man greeted him with a smile on his face. Quincy knew it was impolite not to shake the hand extended towards him, but he had his left hand in his pant pocket, and his car keys in his right hand;(on purpose). After all, he was not there for niceties, and chit-chat. The attorney offered him a chair across from his desk, and then circled around to sit in the leather 'wing-back' chair behind it.

Ron's story did not include the part about him and Donna dating; only that he was investigating something on behalf of a friend. Quincy knew it had to be about Derek, the *coward*.

As it turned out, he and Derek were way off track. They knew none of the particulars. They thought that 'Lizzy' was the child that came from the rape incident. *Quincy wasn't about to soften the word to make it politically correct!*

What was worse, they assumed that Donna would have taken a lot of money to give her daughter up for adoption. His plan was to offer Donna a substantial amount of money, far above what it would cost to adopt a child through legal means, and hope the exclusive sum would keep her mouth shut *to boot*. Maybe that way she wouldn't press charges.

Quincy thought; *the poor fools, they didn't know her character then, and they surly don't know her now.*

If Donna and Quincy wanted to go *that* route, the statute of limitation was well within their favor, but that's not what the Lord spoke to them then, and he wasn't going to change that now. These guys thought their only problem was that after Donna's marriage, they didn't see the child anymore. They had to find out what happened to the child. It seems that after Derek got married, a couple of years in to it, he found that he and his wife were sterile…The both of them! His wife really wanted a child, so naturally he thought *'Why not my own child'?*

Quincy was so angry, he wanted to leap over the desk, and rip Ron's head off. He pressed himself to the seat, and asked God for strength. He needed a drink of water to cool him down, and on Ron's command through the intercom on his desk, one arrived in a few short seconds. Quincy took a few sips of the water, collected himself, and began to relay the true facts to Mr. Baker. He told the *ex-boyfriend* the whole story.

He also made it clear that these heartless *so-and-so's* didn't care about someone else's' life until they needed it to benefit their own. Ron didn't want to believe what he was told, but Quincy told him to go check it out. They (he and Donna) had the law on their side. His wife had a death certificate for the still-born child, a birth certificate for the baby she received in the hospital and adoption papers that proved the natural mother gave her little baby up for adoption that self-same day.

Pastor Folks told him they could produce all the personal data, and official documents that would be needed in a court of law if they wanted to pursue it; however it would do no good, because they no longer had the child. Quincy told Ron he was sure there was certain information that was a matter of public records, like birth announcements and death notices. Those would give him a start if he cared to check it out. When he got up to leave, he stopped half way across the room.

"Oh by the way, I have one more certificate that belongs to me. You might want to check that out too. It's called a marriage license, and I don't know how that works on *this* side of the tracks, but on that side Jordan (he pointed out the window at nothing in particular) I'm king of my castle. And let me make this thing perfectly clear to you; collar, or *no* collar…nobody messes with my queen!"

Having reached for the door, he put his hand on the knob, and turned back to say:

"Don't ever follow, or leave another note for my wife again as long as you live."

Ron who never got up from behind his desk during their conversation (probably because of Quincy's overpowering statue) now stood up.

"That sounds like a threat to me pastor. Don't forget I'm an attorney."

Pastor Folks turned fully around to look Ron square in the eyes, and said,

"Oh trust me *son*. It may sound like a threat, but believe me, it's not. It's a promise! And, I *Mr. Attorney* am being led by an authority that outranks yours by *Eons*. I'm a *Minister* of the most High God!"

He closed the office door behind him, and left his calling card with the receptionist.

TEN

Pastor Q didn't say where he was going, or what his appointment was about this morning, but Donna had a pretty good idea.

She couldn't quite place his mood when he returned, but she knew it was one of those moods where she need not prod him to talk about it. She had less than a year of marriage under her belt, and just because they were Christians, did not mean it was all wedded bliss *all* the time. Some lessons came about the hard way, even though her parents loving marriage never appeared to have any hitches.

Then again, *maybe* that was the only view they let her see.

In one of her marital flair ups she went to search out a resolution form her mother, and found out that her parents had many arguments in their marriage, they just learned how to solve their problems in private. To a child's eyes, it looked like they had a perfect marriage. Mrs. Vaughn's advice to Donna was to become aware of her husband's *'NO YAK'* zone. In other words, she had to learn to love her husband well enough to learn when not to run her 'yap', or try to pick his mind about what was bothering him. Her mother told her:

> "There are just times when men don't want to talk about what is bothering them. They don't want you to help them figure *it* out.
>
> They don't want, or need your advice. It has nothing to do with pride, or male ego. It has nothing to do with if they love you, or not. It's just something they're born with.
>
> It's in them from creation. As a matter of fact, to mess with *those* emotions, might in some way tend to weaken the man."

Mom told me the best thing to do at those times is to be the *good little* helpmate. You pray for whatever it is that is bothering them, and leave well enough alone!

That particular conversation came back to Donna at this time. She sensed the *'man mood'*, and stayed busy with house straightening, and little odd jobs to keep her mind occupied, and her mouth shut!

Quincy tinkered around the house for a while, and then told Donna he was going out for a drive.

That was his *thing!* She wasn't upset, or disturbed about it, because she was beginning to know her husband more and more each day. Some men tinker around in their garage. That's what helps them to think. If they happen to be a musician, they most likely will go play on an instrument. If they are athletic, they will probably go to a gym. It's their time for solitude and peace of mind. She had to understand this had nothing to do with love. It made no difference if the man was married, or single. It's just who they are. Women are natural fixers. The hardest thing for them to do is —not to butt in and try to fix things!

⸻

Pastor Folks returned from his drive with a clear decision not to tell Donna the complete story behind his meeting with the note writer. He knew this was the best thing for now.

He had to wait.

He knew what he would do. He just wasn't sure what Ron Baker had in mind to do. His prayer was that the Lord would move on Ron's heart to have him investigate what he was told.

Quincy couldn't go to his wife to ask her to agree with him in prayer on the matter, so he decided to share what was going on with someone else. It had to be someone he trusted just as much as he trusted his wife; someone he knew would have his best interest at heart, and that someone was his father-in-law. He would ask him after Bible study if he wanted to go out tomorrow for a round of golf.

Quincy wasn't a regular player, but he could hold his own. His father-in-law, on the other hand, was very good. He was retired, and went often with some of the other seniors at the church. When Pastor Folks asked his father-in-law if he wanted to go to the golf course on Thursday, he read right through him. He guessed that Quincy wanted to have a private talk with him. He even suggested that they didn't have to go to the course if he did not want to. But Quincy told him it was okay; he needed the exercise. Besides, it was mid September and the golf course would be closing within the next week or so. This might be his last chance to get out on the course and swing the old clubs.

Donna could only guess that what Quincy told her about the notes was true. And that was that she had a secret admirer.
She didn't want to miss these last two days of work this week. She was a little surprised, but pleased that her husband offered to drive her to work, and pick her up after her shift was over. Donna felt confident that however Quincy handled, or was handling this secret admirer business, it would be decent and in order.

Pastor Q and Donna

When things are going well, you can rest assure the enemy isn't happy, and he'll find a way to come in and disrupt things. She went in to work because she did not want to use too many of her days off. Since she wasn't sick, any days she was using now might come off her vacation days, or personal time off. She used yesterday as a personal day off, and she only had one more for the year.

Donna was thinking ahead. Because Christmas would fall in the middle of the week, the church Cantata was scheduled for the Sunday before Christmas. She wanted to use half her vacation days for Christmas, and the other week for summer vacation. Her husband didn't know it yet, but Donna was looking into doing something they had never done before; go on a cruise.

Christmas was going to be mighty busy with two different homes to visit, her parents, and his family in Wilmington. She had already started to put the Cantata together, and if there were no hitches, everything would come off smoothly. Donna enjoyed working with the little children in her Sunday school class. She even put together a small narrated skit they were going to present for Thanksgiving. The parents were excited about it too. This would be the first time the church would do something other than handing out the Thanksgiving baskets for the needy.

Donna began to reminisce about their first date last year at Christmas time. She remembered how she was swept away by Pastor Folks' thoughtfulness. In any of her *'down times'* the memory of that first date would filter through her mind, and bring joy to her heart, and a smile to her face. She truly hoped that the **Christmas Date** (that's what she named it), would become one of their first traditions they kept as a couple. She knew that later on they would develop family traditions of their own, but for now, since it was just the two of them, they were still very much a part of what each of their families did.

Quincy's game was so far off. A beginner could have beaten him. He apologized to his father-in-law for playing so badly. Deacon Vaughn made a joke saying that maybe the next time (coining one of his wife's phrases), *"they should do lunch!"* Quincy had to laugh.

Deacon Vaughn was a good listener. Quincy respected his wisdom and friendly advice. He may have been the pastor, but everyone needs counsel from those who have wisdom. The two men were basically tuned in to the same thoughts.

Wait was the Word from the Lord!

His father-in-law told him that God had prepared Quincy for any direction the devil would take. If the enemy chose to move to the right, or to the left; he was to remain still and come out the victor! For now, he was to concentrate on being in covenant with his wife.

ELEVEN

Ron Baker did some investigating, and then he put a call in to Pastor Folks. He had his secretary to call the church office. It was the number listed on the business card he left at his office. Evidently, he kept regular office hours at the church on Wednesdays, and Fridays from 9:00am to 1:00pm. The card also had printed information about other church meeting times, and Sunday morning worship, but Ron had no interest in that stuff.

Mrs. Daily buzzed the call through for Pastor Folks. Needless to say, he was a little taken back, but certainly not shocked by the call. Ron wanted to say what he had to say over the phone, however, Quincy convinced him that a face-to-face meeting would be better for the both of them. Maybe Pastor Folks had forgotten that his last words to Mr. Baker were pretty intimidating.

Quincy knew that his calendar was pretty much clear for the day. He did not have any appointments with his parishioners, although he did have a pile of work on his desk that needed his attention, and several phone calls he had to make.

The calls he could make from home, but he needed Mrs. Daily for dictation and to type the letters he needed to get out to other churches. He tried to stay true to the office hours that were on the cards he handed out, because…well, with the amount of growth the church was experiencing, he wanted to be ready for whatever the growth might lead to. And on this particular Friday, it looked like it led to a call from Ron Baker.

When he completed that incoming call, Pastor Folks stepped across the hall to let Mrs. Daily know he was expecting a visitor at about 10:00am. He asked her to do two things for him. One, if she could stay in a mode of prayer for the meeting, and two; to listen out for the bell at the front of the church.

Ron tried to treat this appointment like any other business meeting. He really did not need to bring his attaché case. The few papers he had could have easily been put in the inside front pocket of his Italian brand name designer suit. The attaché case was sort of a security blanket—something to make him look important. When he thought about it, the three-piece suit and attaché case was kind of silly, because his *ego* told him he was already important; at least from a professional point of view.

He rang the bell and waited. Ron hadn't been inside of a church for years, and he surely had never stepped a foot in a '*black*' one. He had to smirk to himself thinking about what he might find.

His only idea of what 'black' church must be like came from old black and white Hollywood movies that showed Negroes as '*next to slavery darkies, shuffling alone saying... 'yez sir Mister boss man'*. As quickly as the thought came, it left.

He knew better than that. He knew these thoughts came from the racist parents he was brought up under. Not any of the Negroes he met, or worked with even came close to what the movies, or TV was portraying. His mind drifted to Donna. He really did like her back then, but he knew his folks would have never allowed her to be a member of *their* family.

The door must have been answered during my musing, because the older woman in the archway seemed to have been repeating her initial greeting to me. She was lovely. She was well dressed, had beautiful salt and pepper hair, and her creamy skin had no need for makeup, although she did wear a touch of lipstick.

Mrs. Daily led the visitor into the church office, and offered him a seat. She rang the code to Pastor Folks' office, and announced the arrival of his appointment. When she hung up the telephone, she told the visitor that *the* pastor would be with him momentarily. Ron was just admiring the secretary's impeccable English, when he heard a door from across the hall, open. The woman stood, and extending her hand towards the office door, said,

"Mr. Baker, Pastor Folks will see you now."

Ron got up from his seat, and took the few steps to face the office entrance. Pastor Quincy stood in the open door of his office. Again, Ron took note of his stature. He extended his hand in a greeting to Ron.

As the two men entered the office, Pastor Folks turned to speak over his shoulder,

"Uh, Mrs. Daily, could you please hold all of my phone calls for the next half hour, or so?"

She tilted her head down looking over the rim of her glasses, as if to say *'what phone calls'?* Then, catching the look on his face, she quickly said,

"Yes, Pastor. I'll make sure you are not disturbed."

At first Ron felt a little intimidated. And, besides that, he still couldn't figure out why they couldn't have taken care of what he had to say over the phone. He was nervous, but after a few minutes, he began to relax.

In the first place, the atmosphere wasn't what he had at all expected. It was quite business-like, not *'churchy'*, if there was such a word. He noticed that the Pastor's demeanor was more friendly than the other day at his office, but, rightly so.

He was on his own turf now, and somewhat calmer. Ron also noticed that the music playing in the background was not gospel. It was soft jazz. *'Well, what do you know*, Ron thought, *this man just might be an ordinary guy under that clergy collar of his'*. He got a check in his mind to *'chill'* out with his attitude.

Because he remembered how wonderful Donna was, he actually felt a twinge of jealously rise up in him against Quincy. He knew that's what he was feeling from the beginning. He even felt it when he was following her around. Ron had really changed over the past few years, and he wished his parent's views would change too. He found that he visited them less and less, because of their prejudices. He told them it was because he was so busy, but he knew differently.

The meeting was over, and he had finished what he came for…to apologize for his actions, and to say that all the information Pastor Folks had given him checked out to the 'Tee'. Ron told Pastor Folks that until Derek approached him, he was not aware that Donna's pregnancy was actually because of his friend's doings, although at times he had his own suspicions.

Ron said he stopped seeing Donna because he thought she lied to him about the rape. He told Quincy the odd thing was— that he broke ties completely with Donna, but Derek was the one who would ask him how she was doing, and if he ever saw her? Ron said after he delivered his findings to Derek yesterday, he dissolved what little was left of their relationship.

Pastor Folks wished him well, and walked him out through the sanctuary to the front doors of the church. On the steps, the two men shook hands, and took a moment to look on each other with an expression that said:

"I believe we understand each other on resolving this issue, and although we may live in the same city, I don't expect that our paths will cross again. We won't call each other friend, but we won't be enemies either."

TWELVE

The autumn days were short lived, and the fall of the year came in beautifully. It was colorful with foliage of turning leaves. There were many shades of browns, oranges, and yellows. The air was crisp and cool, and was usually a welcomed pick-me-up for Donna, but today her spirit was still a bit sluggish. The church was adding another Sunday school class, one that would help to train those adults who believed they had a call on their lives to the *'Five-fold'* ministry that Ephesians 4:11-15, speaks of.

"And he gave some, apostles, and some prophets, and some, evangelist; and some pastors and teachers; For the perfecting of the saints, for the work of the ministry, for the edifying of the body of Christ. Till we all come in the unity of the faith, and of the knowledge of the Son of God, unto a perfect man, unto the measure of the stature of the fullness of Christ: That we *henceforth* be no more children, tossed to and fro, and carried about with every wind of doctrine, by the sleight of men, and cunning craftiness, whereby they lie in wait to deceive; But speaking the truth in love, may grow up into him in all things, which is the head, *even* Christ."

This venture took a lot of effort and long hours in prayer. It wasn't just a matter of selecting someone to go in and teach a class. These were brothers and sisters who were serious about their faith and their commitment to grow. They were willing to make sacrifices to get the training they needed to advance the work of the kingdom of God.

Pastor Quincy was one who stayed in touch with his mother. He called her every week, but because he was also devoting himself to much study and prayer, Donna always checked to see if he remembered to call his mother. They made sure to pay her a visit every month or so, and that visit was scheduled for this coming week. It was just a one-day visit with an overnight stay, but the both of them looked forward to it. Donna enjoyed the company of her mother-in-law as much as she enjoyed visiting with her own parents.

It was mid-October, and after their visit next week, they wouldn't visit her again until Christmas. When she and Pastor Q got married, they started a new family tradition. His mother would visit them for Thanksgiving, and they all would go to the Vaughn's for dinner. When her mother-in-law visited, Donna tried to be the *gracious* host, but she never got a chance to do much hosting. Mother Folks was always doing things around the house, things for Donna, and whatever she could find her hands to do. Donna wanted her to relax. But, Mother Folks loved doing things for her. She said since she never had a daughter, this gave her an opportunity to do a lot of fussy motherly things she couldn't do for the boys.

Donna was feeling a little peaked these days. With the extra push at church, and not wanting to give up any more unscheduled workdays, she decided to forge ahead until November. She still had her two Mondays off a month, and was thinking that after Christmas she would cut back to part-time hours.

The ride down to Wilmington was wonderful. They left immediately after service was over. Neither one of them voiced it, but there seemed to have been a slight weight lifted from their shoulders. The thought of being carefree for the next two days ignited romantic feelings in pastor Q.

"Honey, shall I pull the car over?"

He nodded his head to the right indicating one of the nicer motels.

Donna smiled, and shook her head back and forth. She knew he was just kidding around, but there have been times when he was dead serious.
"Why is it that every time we get in the car for a short road trip, you go to thinking about pulling over to the first motel you see? You would think that we don't have any together time at home."

"Well, you started it."

"Excuse me! Now Quincy you know good- and- well we were on our way home that day, not to a motel."

"Hey. A guy can dream, can't he? Every man has that little thing his wife does that turns him on. And that day when we left my office, and you started to undress in the car…well, that was one of the sexiest things I had ever seen you do.
I guess, ever since then, when we're alone taking a long drive, a feeling of *recklessness* comes over me.
I can't help it. I get flashbacks of that moment when I said…"

Pastor Q and Donna

Donna finished the sentence with him.

"...Don't make me have to stop, and pull this car over."

They started laughing, and Quincy found his wife's hand, brought it to his lips, and gave it a gentle kiss.

"But, when you think about it, you have to admit I'm a pretty strong guy. At least I was able to make it home that day."

"Yeah, just barely!"

These excursions to Mother Folks' were usually just family catching up on things like, who was doing what, and what was going to happen next in their lives. However, this time I had something very personal, and very important to discuss with my mother-in-law. Under normal circumstances, a daughter would discuss something like this with her own mother, but this was not a normal situation. Sharing this with my parents would upset them emotionally just like it's been upsetting me.

Sunday evening was crowded, noisy, and lots of fun. Whenever Mother Folks knew we were coming, it was time for the whole family to get together. She enjoyed cooking a big Sunday dinner. Quincy enjoyed getting together with his brother and his family, and so did I. It was crazy seeing those two brothers together. They told jokes about their childhood. They laughed, carried-on, and acted sillier then the kids. The next morning after breakfast, we girls decided to go shopping, so Quincy could have some alone time. We really went because I wanted to talk with my *second* Mom without any other ears around to hear.

Mom sensed that there was more to this shopping request than just *'girl talk'*. On the drive into town, I hemmed and hawed, and made small 'chit-chat'. All of a sudden, (seemingly out of the blue) Mother Folks cut me off in mid-stream, saying:

"All right, enough of the small talk. You're pregnant, aren't you?"

I was so stunned; I almost ran the red light we were approaching. My hands were frozen to the steering wheel.

"Yes. Yes, and I'm scared to death."

I drove another block or two down the road and turned into the first big shopping center I saw. I pulled in a parking spot, and turned the car off. My shoulders hurt from gripping the wheel so tightly.

Pastor Q and Donna

We decided to stay in the car and talk, because going in the stores and spending money was not going to solve my problem. The sun was shinning warmly through the windshield making the car nice, and toasty. We had eaten breakfast before leaving the house, so why go to a restaurant just to talk. Besides, proprietors want you to patronize their business, not sit in a booth and take up space. The car was okay with both of us.

I loved talking with my mother-in-law. She had an ear to listen, but at times she would cut through the chase, and get you right to the point.

That's not to say that she doesn't show compassion, because she does. She just knows how to appropriate it at the proper time. For someone who has only known me less than a year and a half, she knows me quite well. All I could think about was what happened the first time I got pregnant. My baby came *stillborn*. Everything began to pour out of me.

> "What if it happens again? I don't think I could take it. I've already suffered through two child loses, and I don't want to go through it again. I know God blessed me at that time with Lizzy, but where is she now?"

I knew I was talking crazy, but she let me ramble on anyway.

> "I know Quincy wants children. I want a child too, but I know there are other ways to obtain children. There are plenty of babies and children out there in

need of adoption. Believe me I know, because I've gone that route. My...my problem is..., (Donna began to cry) I'm already pregnant, and I'm trying not to have negative thoughts about it. I feel stuck, and I don't know what to do."

When mother Folks spoke, her voice was calm and steady.

"Have you gone to the doctor's yet?"

"No, but I'm pretty sure I'm between six, and seven weeks along."

"Well, let me tell you first what I think. I believe there are strands of uncertainty running through your mind at this time, and the longer you entertain the spirit of fear, the more of his buddies come in to join the party.

You've said a lot of I's. I, this, and I that. You're already on the brink of selfishness. The Bible says in 2 Timothy 1:7,

> "For God hath not given us the spirit of fear, but of power, and of love, and of a sound mind."

Just in that scripture alone, we can see some of the works the Lord has intended us to have: Power, Love, and A Strong Mind.
So, that is what the enemy will attack. In some of his craftiness he may use stress, doubt, fear of death, or

dying, torment, anxiety, and pain just to name a few. From listening to you, I guess that you have already experienced a few of these symptoms."

"Yes, I have. But, I didn't think that they had anything to do with the fears I was having."

"Believe me child, when the devil comes in, he doesn't come alone! His job is to steal, kill, and to *destroy*."

"Wow! I don't know what to say. Just hearing what you said makes me angry. As a matter of fact, at the moment, I feel more angry than afraid. I also fell silly for not fully recognizing the enemy."

"Well, that's only the beginning. Donna, I know you didn't have it in your heart to do Satan's work for him.

"Wait, wait. What do you mean by me doing Satan's work for him?"

"What I mean is what we just said; that his work was to steal, kill, and to destroy, and ours is to have Love, Power, and a strong Mind. These are attributes that help us to advance the kingdom of God, not to destroy it."

Mrs. Folks took her daughter-in-laws hand and placed it in hers.

"First we'll pray asking for forgiveness, and then we'll agree in prayer to bind the Spirit of Fear, and its works. At the same time we have to agree on what you want God to loose in your life. We'll start with 2Timothy 1:7, and then add some *I Am's* to the mix."

"Some I Am's. What are they?"

"They are reminders of who we are in Christ, and what He expects us to be in His strength.

For example, He expects us to believe in the divine victory over everything He went to the cross for. He expects you to remember that you are redeemed from the curse of the law of sin and death. That can be put in the form of an '*I am*' statement. Here's another one. '*I am firmly rooted, built up, established in my faith and overflowing with thanksgiving.*' That's from Colossians 2:7."

"Mother Folks, thank you so much. I never thought of using scripture in that way. Believe it or not, I can already feel the cloud lifting from my gloominess."

"Donna, I was a pastor's wife for more that thirty years. I went into it as fresh and new as you are today, but I was determined to make my marriage, and his ministry work. Over the years God has shown me many things about being a helpmate."

"Mom, can I ask your advice on one more thing?"

"Sure. Ask on!"

"Just talking with you has made me realize it probably was in my heart to have this baby anyway, and like you say, I allowed fear of the unknown to take over my thoughts. But do you think it will be okay if I keep this from Quincy for a little while longer?"

"I guess that's your choice since it looks like you may have a particular reason for waiting."

"Yes, and I've just now thought of it. I'm going to make an appointment with the doctor, so I can get on tract to having a healthy pregnancy and a beautiful baby. If my timing is right, I won't be showing for a while, so I want to hold off telling him, so I can announce it as his 'Christmas surprise'. That is if morning sickness doesn't give me away first."

The two ladies laughed, and Mrs. Folks said:

"Well, we'll just have to agree in prayer for that too. That isn't a hard thing for the Lord to do. After all nothing ... (Donna chimed in with her mother-in-law to finish the sentence) is impossible with God!"

THIRTEEN

Donna was grateful for more than just having talked with her mother-in-law about her dilemma. Mrs. Folks promised to call her daughter-in-law more often, but not enough to arouse suspicion on the part of her son.

Donna was glad to have someone other than her own mother to confide in.

She was learning one thing. It was okay to keep her mother informed on some things, but sharing too much about her personal life with Quincy wasn't such a good idea. He was her husband, but too much negative of *anything* about him could even affect their thoughts of him as their pastor. It was nice to have someone else to turn to when she felt overwhelmed as a pastor's wife. She had heard a lot of bad *'mother-in-law'* stories from coworkers, and other people, and felt truly blessed that that was not the case with her.

⌒

By the end of October through mid November only small bouts of morning sickness had arisen...nothing too serious, maybe their prayers were being answered. She had heard that every pregnancy was a little different from the previous one, and she was thankful. The episodes of morning sickness she did have seemed to have gone unnoticed by her husband. Of course it was helpful that she got up to start her day earlier than Quincy had to get up to start his.

Donna was getting excited about keeping her secret. Another thing working in her favor was the seasonal weather. It was the fall of the year. It wasn't time for overcoats yet, but the changing weather did call for heavy sweaters, or layering with a small jacket, or cape.

That was the good part. The not so good part was that *'intimacy'* was her husband's middle name. *Maybe not so good is not the right word she thought.* I love his attention, and flirtation. Some of his advances extend into the bedroom, and some are just to let me know how much he loves me. The way he puts it is...*how much he appreciates God sending him his* **'good thing'**.

Both of our schedules at church were busy. Pastor Quincy was working with the new Sunday school class, and the deacons who were organizing the *'Bringing In the Sheaves'* food drive. The whole thing started as an *in-house* ministry several years ago. The effort was to provide enough food for a Thanksgiving dinner for needy families in the congregation. From that small effort, it has now spread to become an outreach into the entire community.

The church provides Thanksgiving boxes for as many families as they can serve.

I was helping with the senior's ministry, and with the Sunday school. This year we're putting together a skit to be presented on the Sunday before Thanksgiving. I know children have history lessons in school about the Pilgrims, but it doesn't hurt to present some of that history from a Christian point of view; you know; *through insurmountable obstacles, God still provides!*

I was also over the Christmas pageant.

Since Christmas falls on a Friday this year, the pageant would be held on the Sunday before Christmas, which is the 20th of December. For that reason, there wasn't much time between the two presentations. With Christmas being that far down in the week, we could have scheduled the pageant for Christmas Day, or on the following Sunday, but then we would run into the problem of having families that would be out of town for the holiday.

I had to begin practice for the Christmas pageant while still practicing for the Thanksgiving presentation.

Being that busy was bound to have an effect on me in the romance department.

It wouldn't be so bad as long as we both agreed that less intimacy was okay for a while. It's not like we didn't have enough romance in our lives to sustain a loving relationship for a couple of weeks. And if it led to an unexpected encounter in the bedroom; well, so be it. We *are* husband and wife. I just wanted to hide my slightly bulging mid-section a little while longer, so I could keep my surprise for just the right moment.

The Thanksgiving basket give-away turned out to be a great witnessing tool. Even before the boxes were to be handed out on the Monday and Tuesday before Thanksgiving, some of the families attended service on the Sunday and Wednesday before Thanksgiving. Many people were so appreciative of our outreach that they wanted to give something back. If all they could give back was their presence, then they wanted to share the Lord's Day with us.

When we knocked on doors in the community, we didn't know what we would find. Some homes didn't need a Thanksgiving box, but wanted to donate money and other goods to help the cause. We went out to bless others, and the church ended up getting blessed all the more. One of our senior couples came across a family who had just moved to the area. Not only did they need our help, they were also looking for a place to worship. I guess you never know why God prompts you to do certain things. The main thing is to be obedient, and let Him do the rest.

Pastor Q and Donna

Mother Folks came down on the Wednesday before Thanksgiving. Quincy and I told her she did not have to bring anything, just to bring herself, but as you can imagine that request went unheeded. Our household was to prepare the turkey, glazed ham, potato salad (my specialty), and Quincy's famous stuffing (ha, ha). Mother Folks was making a sour cream pound cake. My folks were doing the rest of the fixing's. I enjoy having my mother-in-law in the house. We really work well together. I wanted to spend as much time with her as I could.

I worked first shift on Wednesday from 7:00a to 3:00p. I used the last of my personal days off, on the Friday after Thanksgiving. That gave me Thursday through Sunday off. I still had seven days left of my ten day paid vacation period, and three sick days, I hoped I didn't have to use. Of course everything closes out at the end of the year, but who knows what I would need to use before then.

I knew from my first pregnancy that I really didn't start to show until about my fifth or sixth month. I'm lucky I guess. So, maybe I can keep this hidden long enough to be the gift that Quincy has wanted for such a long time.

I thank God he is a man that believed in waiting for the right woman to marry, and stayed abstinent in his waiting. He said he just didn't believe in ruining it for another man who was looking for...*someone who was saving herself just for him.*

When Quincy asked me what I wanted for Christmas, I told him I'd like to go to that festive Amish diner theatre restaurant he took me to on our first date.

That's not only when he tricked me into saying *'yes'* to our first date, but that's also when I realized I was falling in love with him.

Since the Christmas Cantata will be on December 20th, I'll take that week off for my vacation.

I love Christmas!

Actually in my thinking, Christmas is not just the short season that's posted on the calendar; it's all year round. I start it early, and end it late, but it doesn't come to an end in our home, or in my heart.

Anyone who comes in our home will see a little bit of Christmas all year long. If they look hard enough they'll see an appliquéd plaque in the kitchen that reads *'God Bless Our Home At Christmastime'*. I have a metallic purple garland rope that hangs over the doorway entering the house from the garage, and there is always a carved *Nativity* scene somewhere.

Aside from the planned gift I'm giving my husband (a new clergy robe), I'm trying to think of a neat way to give him a present that will give him a hint of the forthcoming addition to our family. I've been racking my brain, but I haven't thought of anything yet. But, whatever it is I find, I want him to wonder ... *"What kind of crazy gift is this?"*

FOURTEEN

As much as I love the Christmas season, I must admit I had very little decorations of my own to decorate with. Up until I married Quincy (less than a year ago) I was living at home with my parents. Their house was always festive, but those things belonged to them, even if I did purchase a few of them. Those decorations belonged to their household now. Besides, how cinchy would it be for me to take Christmas decorations back from my parents?

Quincy had a few things, but nothing to elaborate, because he always spent Christmas with his family every year too. It's funny how people always think of the essentials they'll need when they get married; you know—furniture, appliances, cooking utensils, and linen, but who thinks of something like Christmas decorations? I know I didn't.

Now, I found myself so busy with everything else I was doing, that decorating the house didn't enter into my mind until I thought about Mother Folks coming for Thanksgiving. I wanted to have a few things out when she came. She probably was finished decorating the inside of her house by now, and waiting on Quincy's brother to come over to help with the outside.

We were in the supermarket shopping for what we needed to get to complete our part of the Thanksgiving meal, and seeing so much *Christmas* in the store; it must have hit both of us at the same time. Wow! Where had our minds been? On the way to the checkout, we laughed about it.

"I guess", Quincy said, "We're use to spending Christmas with our Folks, and their homes are already decorated."

"I guess so", I said. "But, you know, maybe we could pick up a few things while we're here."

"I'll tell you what. Why don't you stay in line with the shopping cart, and I'll go down the other aisle to see what I can find."

Pastor Q and Donna

Then he looked up the line past the register and said,

"Why don't we start with those?"

He was pointing to rows of beautiful poinsettia plants across the front of the store. The plants were lining the inside and outside windowsills. Quincy went to pick out two giant red plants, and sat them at the end of the cashier stand of the line we were in. He had such a big grin on his face when he got back to the cart. He was well pleased.

"Now", he said, rubbing his hands together. "Honey, I'm going to run right down that aisle over there to see if I can find some twinkle lights. I'll be right back."

He looked like a little boy on Christmas morning, his face beaming from ear to ear. He came back with an arm full of *everything*.

"What in the world is all that for?"

"Oh yeah", he said. "Forgot about the food in the cart, I guess I'd better get one of those carrier *thing-ies*."

When he came back from up front, he apologized to the lady who was standing behind me. I was scared to look back to see the expression on her face. But, his pleasant apology must have won him favor, because she replied in a very sweet tone,

"Oh that's all right, it's not a problem."

I could only imagine if that had been me, or any other woman for that matter, who kept adding things to her basket while she was already standing in the checkout line. I'm almost positive the response would have been quite different. Quincy was in the middle of telling me something, when I stopped thinking about what the woman would have said to me.

"...and, these are for the outside shrubs under the living room window, and this lighted garland is for the outside stair railing. Look honey, it's made of plastic, so it'll hold up in the weather. When we get up to the register, I want to get about four, or five of those smaller poinsettias to put between the shrubs, and one on each side of the entry door."

He was jabbering so fast, I could hardly keep up with what he was saying.

"Quincy. What are you talking about?"

"Why, the outside of the house of course. Won't that arrangement look great? I've got it all planned out. I thought I'd get the outside decorated first, and then we can work together on the inside."

"And you thought of this whole plan in the two minutes it took you to go down that aisle, and come back."

"No. Not entirely. Some of it I've wanted to do for a long time."

"Look here Pastor Folks, (I leaned in to whisper to him) some of the people in this grocery store are working within a budget…and I just happen to be one of them!"

He knew he was in trouble when Donna went from 'honey' to 'Pastor Folks'. He realized he was getting a bit carried away. Donna didn't want to disappoint him, so she thought of something that could give him the same effect he wanted, but without exhausting their entire budget.

"Hey, why don't we do this? Keep the twinkle lights, and the garland for the outside, and the two large poinsettias for the inside of the house. Then when we leave here, we can swing around to the *'Five and Ten'* discount store on the way home. We can pick up some of those artificial poinsettias for the outside.

We'll save money, and we can use them again for as many years as you want to."

Pastor Folks leaned over the cart to plant a kiss on his wife's forehead.

"Thanks honey. That's a great idea."

He moved from standing beside the buggy to stand in back of his wife. He leaned in, and whispered behind the lobe of her ear,

"I'm so glad I married you. You're not only fine, and I do mean *fine*, but you're smart to boot."

Donna could feel he was getting too close, so she purposely let her left foot swing back, and gave him a gentle kick in the shin. She turned around in time to see his sequenced up face from her unexpected kick. With a slight smile on her face and whispering between clinched teeth she said,

"You are in a public place Pastor Folks. It's our turn next. So, maybe you can offer a hand by starting to put some of these groceries on the counter."

Pastor Q and Donna

Donna wasn't really peeved at him, but she knew how her husband could be if she didn't put clamps on his actions right then.

They stopped by the local 'Five and Ten' to pick up the artificial poinsettias and a few other decorative items. Before they got out of the car, Donna reached over to give her husband a kiss. They lingered there just a couple of minutes. She hoped that would make amends for her keeping him at bay in the grocery store. It did.

She smiled to herself as they walked through the door hand and hand. Donna wasn't sure what stimulated his emotions more at that moment; her kisses, or Christmas shopping, but she believed she was slowly losing out to Christmas shopping. They picked up the things they needed, and were out of the store in about twenty minutes.

Quincy brought in the groceries. I emptied the bags and made room for everything in the refrigerator and the cabinets. I told him I would pull together something for us to eat for dinner. He was so anxious to get started on his decorating I didn't have the heart to ask him to wait until after we had eaten.

Until we purchased the things we got this evening, our combined decoration consisted of a kitchen plaque, the small porcelain nativity scene, a purple garland cord

I found at a garage sale, and a few other things Quincy had in a box up in the attic. My husband always said how much he loved the Christmas season, and I guess the joy of it becomes even greater when you have someone to share it with.

Quincy came in once to get another extension cord. I reminded him we should eat soon. He told me he was almost finished. Actually I might have been hungrier than he was, because I was with him most of the day, and wasn't able to sneak in the extra snack I usually eat. He was true to his word. He popped in the door not more than ten minutes later, and invited me to come out and look at his masterpiece. It was truly beautiful, although the poinsettias were hard to see because it had gotten dark. I was sure it would look better in the light of day.

After we had dinner, he was ready to pull out the rest of the things, and get started on the inside. To tell the truth, I was a little fatigued, but he was so hyped up about decorating, and we only had a few things to put up anyway. We added the old with the new, and before we knew it; the house was looking more festive.

Of course it was nothing to compare with either one of our parent's home, but it was a good start. We had not decided if we were going to get a tree, or not. We had to think that one through, because it wasn't just a matter of the tree, but also a matter of purchasing decorations to go on it. This was our first Christmas as Pastor and wife, and I knew Quincy wanted to bless the church.

Pastor Q and Donna

We really wanted to be a blessing in the toy give-a-way, and he also wanted to be a financial blessing to those who volunteered their services on a weekly basis to the ministry. He receives a salary, and the only other person who got paid on a weekly basis was the janitorial service that cleaned the church. Quincy wanted those who worked faithfully in the ministry every week volunteering their service, to know how much they were appreciated. He wanted to give them a heartfelt bonus of *'Thanks'*.

FIFTEEN

There's never a good time for bad news. And, there is no such thing as getting use to hearing about death, no matter how often it comes. It still is a shock.

Sister Richardson and her husband Willie visited family over the Thanksgiving weekend. I called her on the Saturday evening before church, as I usually did, to see if she was planning to go to service. If she was (this Sunday), I had to allow some extra time in my morning routine in order to swing around and pick her up, or I would have to ask my parents to get her. The good thing about picking her up for church is that I never had to wait on her. She was always ready; peeking out of the window, or listening for the car in the driveway.

Since Mother Folks was staying over for service, she would either have to ride with Quincy, or drive her own car if I needed to pick her up. But, Sister Richardson said she was not going to church this Sunday. She told me that after they got in from their family gathering, her husband was feeling a little poorly, and since he hadn't fully recovered, she thought she'd better stay home and keep an eye on him. She asked if we would say an extra prayer for them at the altar, and I told her we would.

After service was over, I followed Quincy to his office because I wanted to call the Richardson's to see how things were going. When there was no answer, I knew something was wrong. My parents, my mother-in-law, and the two of us had planned to go out to dinner after church, but sensed it was the Lord who directed us to go over to the Richardson's first. We knocked, and there was no answer. The neighbor who lived across the street saw our cars in the driveway, and came over to tell us that we just missed them by fifteen or twenty minutes. He said Mrs. Richardson, and her brother-in-law had taken Mr. Willie to the hospital. Without even discussing it, we turned our cars around, and headed straight for Lancaster General. Quincy used his clergy pass for parking, and we all went in to the emergency desk.

Mr. Richardson was still being attended to in the emergency area down the corridor. Mom, Dad, and Mrs. Folks took some seats in the emergency room waiting area, and Quincy and I went on down the hall to locate the room. He felt for my hand as we walked, and I knew he was praying. I relaxed a little knowing the section we were directed to was not the Trauma, or critically injured unit, but that didn't mean the situation was not serious. Mr. Willie was still in the examining process.

We peeped through the slightly parted curtains to view Sister Richardson sitting in a chair next to his bed. Pastor Quincy cleared his throat to get her attention. The look on her face could only be described as the look of relief one has when their pastor walks through the door.

I moved in quickly to give her a loving hug. Pastor patted her on the back, and moved to the opposite side of the bed. Mr. Richardson was hooked up to IV's, a heart monitor, breathing apparatus, and had an oxygen tent across the top portion of his body.

He was pretty much incapacitated being strapped to the bed in several places, but he managed to give Quincy an acknowledging blink with his eyes. He reached under the tent for Mr. Richardson's hand, and gave it a gentle squeeze. We had only been in the room a few minutes when the doctor and attending nurse come in to speak with Sister Richardson about some of the results from his x-rays. She introduced us and said that she would like for her pastor to be in on whatever was being said. They agreed and headed towards the curtain that separated the room from the hallway.

Pastor Quincy said he would like just a moment with Mr. Richardson, for prayer, and he would be on directly. In those extra moments he took Mr. Willie's hand, and prayed the prayer of Salvation with him. He asked him to squeeze his hand if he wanted to renew his faith in Christ. When Pastor Quincy felt the light squeeze of his hand, he asked him to affirm his belief by doing the best he could to confess it verbally. With the breathing tube in his mouth, the best Mr. Willie could do was to grunt through slightly parted lips. Pastor Folks asked him if that was a *'yes'*, and he nodded his head down to his chest and back up again in affirmation of his answer. Tears began to stream out the corner of his eyes, and Pastor Quincy spoke up loudly so he could hear:

"Then welcome back my brother into the family of Christ."

He then left out of the room to meet up with those who were waiting for him in the corridor.

In a more secluded area, the doctor said they were still waiting on some more test results, but for now they were sure that he had a severe case of double Pneumonia. One lung had collapsed completely, and the other was pretty weak. The doctor said he was almost certain that the illness came on him so rapidly because of his bronchitis, and weak lungs. He was in the wheelchair do to the heart attack and stroke he suffered almost three years ago. He never fully recovered.

Since they were still in the process of admitting him, we prayed a short prayer with Beverly so she could get back to her husband. When she was out of earshot, the doctor pulled me aside to tell me the situation didn't look to promising. Christians have to be careful with what they fall in agreement with, but there had already been a check in my spirit that confirmed what the doctor was saying. That's why the Lord led me the way He did.

Pastor Q and Donna

When Pastor Q and Donna got back to the waiting room, they filled the others in on what was happening. Except; Pastor Folks didn't fill them in on what was between him and the Lord. Some things the Lord will put in a pastor's bosom to be released for a later time; and other things may stay there for eternity. That's part of the call of the mantle.

It was nearly three O'clock, and we still had not eaten. I suggested we go to one of the local buffet restaurant in the area. Most of the crowd that came in right after their services ended had pretty much cleared out by now. I knew it would be getting on towards five O'clock by the time we left the buffet. Our original plans had shifted putting us about two hours behind how we thought the day would go. With that in mind I suggested for Mom to spend the night, and head back home in the morning.

SIXTEEN

Mom woke up early the next morning to fix us a good hearty breakfast. The night before when she said that was what she wanted to do, we tried our best to talk her out of it, but you can imagine how that went. This was Donna's Monday off, and with everything that was going on, I was ready to sleep in. I don't believe that neither one of us slept well because of what was on our minds, and in our hearts.

I notified Mrs. Daily of the situation when we got home, and asked her to call one of the couples in the Deacons' Ministry to visit the hospital in the morning as soon as they could. I was pretty sure that Sister Richardson had spent the night there.

    Deacon Allen and his wife was the couple that went to the hospital. The call came in about a half hour after Mother Folks left for home. Mr. Willie had passed. Donna and I went straight to the hospital.
    Mr. Willie's brother was there when we arrived. He said he was leaving for the house, and would call family members from there. I called Mrs. Daily, and she was ready to notify as many church members as she could get in touch with. The Ladies' Auxiliary would arrange to bring food and drinks over to Sister Richardson's house for family who would be coming in during the day.
    It didn't take long before the neighbors were aware of Beverly Richardson's loss, and they were willing to do whatever they could do to ease her grief.

    Once the family began to filter in, I checked in with Sister Richardson. Her sister from out of town, and Mr. Willie's brother would be handling everything from writing the Obituary to whatever was needed for the funeral and internment.

    By Wednesday evening we made an announcement to the entire congregation. There might have been some members who were not contacted, or maybe had not seen the write up in the Obituaries of the local newspaper. We now knew the funeral would be on Saturday, December 2nd. Mrs. Daily worked with the family in planning the

Pastor Q and Donna

outline of the service, and would see that bulletins were run off at the printers.

This would be a very moving occasion for me, but if anything good, or rewarding was to come out of it, I had shared with Sister Beverly on one of my pastoral visits what occurred between her husband and the Lord those few minutes I stayed behind in the hospital room. She was so pleased to hear that news, and it seemed as if a weight had been lifted from her shoulders. She was still grieving, but not as one without hope.

We entered the month of December with a few unexpected turns. Mourning with my friend for her loss was one of them. The other was a nice Christian jester extending from the Allen's visit to the hospital.

They stayed that day until we got to the hospital, and they waited around until Sister Richardson was ready to leave. They, of course, offered to see that she got home safely. Much to their surprise, the Allen's found out that they lived not more than a five-minute drive from her house.

Sister Allen knew that was one of the extra things I did for the *Household of Faith,* and she and her husband volunteered to see that Sister Richardson got back and forth to church whenever she wanted to go. She said she and her husband were looking for another way to help out in the church. She even was going to stop by at least once during the week to run errands for her, or to take her along if she just wanted to get out of the house.

I really love the people of God.

It dawned on me that God was meeting my needs before the prayer request was made. I was willing to keep up with my pledge to assist Mother Richardson, but in the infinite wisdom of Who He is, God knew that for me to continue to work, handle the Christmas program, and stay healthy in my present condition, would prove to be too much stress on me and maybe the baby too.

I may have gotten past morning sickness okay, but I was doing poorly when it came to my cravings. It didn't do any good to keep my pregnancy weight down, when I was the culprit behind my other weight gain. But, I guess that comes along with the territory!

I really had it bad for any candy bar that had nuts in it. And, those trips to get those special quarter pound charbroiled hamburgers weren't doing me any good either. I was about four months along, and the bathroom scale let me know I was gaining weight a little too rapidly. The doctor said I wasn't that much off track, but if I felt that way, I should be careful, and do things (I knew he meant eating the hamburgers) in moderation. It could have been my salt intake he said, that was causing the swelling.

At home, I didn't want to rouse any suspicion, so I kept my prescribed vitamins and daily supplement tablets at work. The ones I would need for the three days I would be at home, I kept in a pouch in my pocket book. I wished I could make time fly to hurry this pregnancy along; not to make the baby come any faster, but so I wouldn't feel so guilty about keeping it from my husband. I guess it was one of those *'bad'*, good ideals that we experience from time to time. Lord, help me get through this!

SEVENTEEN

After a loved one dies, family and friends are a welcomed solace, but eventually they have to get back to their own lives.

I knew there was plenty of family surrounding Sister Richardson for the moment, so I saved my visit for the week after family went back home. I called a couple of times, and I knew she was being taken care of very well.

It was wonderful to hear how much she and the Allen's were getting along. It was also nice to have a visit where I could just come and sit with my friend. The talk was slow with much reminiscing in between. I shared some consoling thoughts with her, and I really felt led to share with her about our expecting a baby.

The old folks say that death makes room for another life.

I told her that I was waiting to tell my husband, but I thought God didn't mind me sharing it with her first. She said my secret was safe with her, and she was honored to be a part of something that reached into her future. She said it made her feel good that a new life was coming into the world.

⸻

Since regular choir rehearsal was on Saturday mornings, the children would also rehearse for the Christmas pageant. The 'senior' ladies were busy making costumes, and the 'senior' men were helping out with building the scenery. The small children practiced their speeches, and the older youth learned their lines for the pageant. Everything was coming together nicely.

The Couple's Ministry was in charge of decorating the church for Christmas, and the Single's were to oversee the refreshments and the toy give-a-way for the children on the night of the pageant.

Rita Whitley signed up to participate. She had already signaled out a few of the unmarried, late twenty to thirty year old men in the congregation and was doing a fair-market job of getting them to participate in the event.

I guess to show off her talent and abilities in certain areas, she volunteered to assist them in baking cookies (at their house, or hers), and to go shopping with them to find the correct *age*-appropriate toy for children in a certain age group.

One could only guess that while she was shopping for the child, she was also shopping for herself.

I mentioned it to Pastor Q, but he didn't see any need to interfere. What harm could it do? He felt that as long as the males were of age, and could make their own decisions, it was up to them if they took her up on her offer. He even laughed about it in a jokingly sort of way saying,

> "Maybe more of our members ought to be like Rita. At least she's determined to reach personal goals she's set for herself. It's true she may not use an orthodox approach to what she does, but at least she's creative!"

Both of our schedules were getting full, and a little more hectic, so it was to be expected that we began to run out of steam. We cooked less, and sent out more. The deli was becoming our best friend.

In order to throw off any oncoming suspicion about what I knew was going on with me; I commented that it appeared like both of us were putting on a little weight. It was the truth. Quincy said he could tell he had put on a few pounds, but he wasn't about to go on a diet now; not with Christmas just around the corner. He said he was thinking about all those Christmas cakes, and other goodies he's been waiting to sample. He wanted to enjoy the holiday, and let loose a little. However, he did mention he thought the Lord was nudging him towards a fast, and maybe the first of the year would be a good time to start.

We often went on a fast together. One of the things I appreciate about my husband is that just because he hears from the Lord to go on a fast, he doesn't automatically assume it is meant for the both of us. He usually asks me if I want to join with him, or he will ask me if I was hearing the same thing from the Lord. If I had the same quickening in my spirit, there was no question that we were to fast together for whatever the Lord was preparing us for.

I returned to work after Thanksgiving, and was sitting in my office having *another* bite to eat, and reflecting on the family gathering. When I thought about it, I wasn't so sure my secret was completely hidden from everyone. When we were at my parent's house for Thanksgiving dinner, I remember looking up every now and then to see my mother giving me an odd glance.

While we were in the kitchen putting the food into serving bowls, she asked me if I was feeling all right. I told her yes; and backed it up with, maybe a little tired from the rehearsals for the play, cooking, and decorating the house. I told her the Pastor and I realized that when his mother was coming down, we didn't have much up in the way of Christmas decorations, so when we went shopping for the food, and we purchased a few decorations to make the house look more festive.

She agreed all of those doings could indeed tire a person out and said,

"I don't see why you young folks want to do so many things at one time. One of these days burning the candle at both ends is going to catch up with you."

And, then she added, while looking at me in an under-eyed glance;

"That is, if it hasn't already."

I don't think she was fooled at all by my excuses. Mothers and Mother-in-laws have a second sense when it comes to the *B-a-b-y* thing!

The next day was my short day at work. I only worked until 11:00a. I felt like making a pot of soup for the household, and thought that would be just the thing to take with me to Sister Beverly when I visited her this afternoon. The soup was still cooking when Quincy left the house. The 'seniors' were coming over to the church to work on their assignments for the Christmas play. It made no sense for the ladies to come one day, and for the men to come another day since most of the husbands were the drivers anyway. They called it 'killing two birds with one stone'. A couple of the older women said they would bring their sewing machines, and the other ladies would cut out the patterns.

I made two small pans of cornbread, and everything was finished around two o'clock. I dipped up some hot soup and put it in a large Pyrex bowl. Before I put the top on, I covered the bowl with plastic wrap, and then put the soup in the quilted soup carrier. I sat the small pan of cornbread on top of the soup bowl. I figured to have about two hours for the visit with Sister Richardson. That way Quincy and I should get back home at about the same time.

Sister Richardson was so glad to see me, and I was glad to see her. We had talked on the phone, but as usual she was glad to see me. I sat the soup and cornbread on the back of the stove, and told her everything was ready, and all she had to do was to dip some into a bowl when she was ready. She asked if I would put everything in the oven for her, and turn the dial on low, that way everything would stay warm while we talked. I removed the plastic wrap from the soup, and put the lid back on. I placed the items in the oven on low, and joined her in the living room. I loved when my elders gave me little tit bits of instructions like that. But sometimes it makes me wonder … "Why didn't I think of that?"

EIGHTEEN

Since we wanted to be a blessing in the toy give-a-way, Quincy and I decided to forgo purchasing a Christmas tree this year. That in return would also eliminate the extra expense of buying ornaments and other trinkets we would need to decorate it with.

We decided we would do it for next year, and the best way to get a head start on *next* year's Christmas was to catch the after Christmas clearance sales *this* year.

By the time the second and third weeks of January roll around, all the Christmas stuff should be marked down by fifty to seventy-five percent off. The retailers would be clearing their shelves to make room for Valentines' Day displays.

We try to work within a budget, mostly paying cash for what we purchased. I always put back a small portion of my paycheck and Quincy's salary for incidentals and emergencies. I use from that money rather than going into the household budget to purchase non-essentials.

Quincy was pleased that I cut some of my work hours back. It gave us more time together and better opportunities to get things done for the ministry. Sometimes when I got off early, he'd plan for us to take a drive somewhere, or we would cook dinner together, and just sit around and relax.

I now worked every other Monday (as usual), Tuesdays from 3:30p — to 11:30p; a half day on Wednesday. I'm off on Thursdays, and worked Fridays from 7:00a — to 3:00p. I couldn't give the hospital any notice of my leaving yet, because I would have to give them some kind of reason, and I sure wasn't going to tell them anything about being pregnant before I said something to my husband. I knew I would be taking an extended maternity leave when I did decide to give notice. I just hadn't decided if I was going to return, or not.

On my day off, we slept in, and then Quincy planned for us to go Christmas shopping for the toy give-a-way. I liked when he planned things for us to do. It seems like every since we were dating, he had a pretty good idea of what I would like, and where I would like to go. Actually we had decided to purchase several toys to add to what the 'single's were rallying for the church to do.

They were only chairing the project. It looked like it was coming along well, but Quincy (as Pastor) wanted to be confident that every child would receive a present. Everyone was doing what they were asked to do. Some decided to go a step farther. For instance, the Deacons were purchasing about fifty, or so knitted skull hats that could be worn by boys and girls alike. Their wives were going to match that effort by purchasing sets of knitted gloves and scarves.

We were excited about the enthusiasm that was spreading throughout the congregation. If anything was a challenge, it was keeping the extras from the kids. Our secret donation was going to be a filled Christmas stocking for everyone. You know the kind that the manufactures put out. We hoped we had enough saved up to get one for each adult too. We knew we'd probably have to go to several stores in order to get enough for the whole church. We weren't a large congregation, but we were growing.

Quincy was beaming with excitement, and to tell the truth, so was I. Our first stop was to the local Five 'n Ten were we often traded. It was during the day, so the store wasn't what you call busy-busy. School was still in.

The store manager and the regular workers knew our faces. I say regular workers, because there was a new face or two behind counters, and working in the aisles. The store must have hired on a couple of extra workers for the holidays. We wanted to buy as many of the stockings as we could, but we didn't want to clean the rack out completely. Suppose someone else came in looking to buy a stocking for his or her child. We definitely wanted to keep that in mind.

The store manager must have noticed we were gathering up a lot of stockings, and came over to see what was going on. Quincy explained that we were buying the stockings for our Christmas give-a-way at church. The manager seemed interested. He tapped the side of his face with his finger, and asked us if we could wait where we were for a minute, he'd be right back.

He returned saying, he didn't know how many stockings we needed, but he made a call to his district manager, and maybe the store could do better than wholesale for what we needed. That sounded good to our ears, because we weren't even thinking that we could get the stockings at wholesale price. So, I thought, anything better than wholesale had to save us a bunch of money. The only thing was we had to get the entire unit.

We didn't have any idea how many stockings were in the unit, but we agreed. He wrote something on a piece of paper, and handed it to the young boy working behind the counter. He asked him to find the box with that stock number on it, and bring it to the floor. Meanwhile, he told us we were just about to be blessed.

Evidently his store and a couple of others had not completed their annual donations to charities. They had already given to the Salvation Army, a children's home, and still had some dollars to go before they met their annual quota of donation write-offs. I heard him talking, but I still knew what our budget was.

He took us upstairs to the office so we could fill out the necessary form. I guess it was customary if a charitable institution was receiving such a large discount. Quincy filled in the church name, location, and telephone number. He signed his name as the party receiving the merchandise. The line under his name was to be signed by a witness. To the right of those two lines were two more lines. The store manager signed the top line, and the lady at the desk; of whom I presumed was the store clerk, signed her name under his. We stood there waiting, because we still had not been quoted a price. The manager shook Quincy's hand, and said:

"Congratulations Pastor Folks". Then heading towards the door he said,

"I thought I heard you folks talking about getting some toys."

We were grateful for what he was doing, but our budget would only go so far. I flashed my eyes at Quincy.

"Well sir, it's just that…well you see, we want to see what our balance on the stockings comes to first before we venture into anything else."

The store manager let out a little laugh, and slapped Quincy on the back. Quincy gave him a puzzled look.

"Excuse me Parson; I guess I didn't fully explain myself. I forgot when I left off I was talking to you about a discount, but when I made my phone call, I was reminded that you were to be the other charitable institution we needed to give to make our quota. There's no charge for the Christmas stockings. You don't owe us a cent. And, if you can shop for the other toys you wanted, and bring the cost in under $100.00 dollars, we'll go downstairs and get started."

We were flabbergasted! This was *s-o-o-o*...God. Quincy asked me to do the shopping, and I was glad to oblige. This was right up my alley! I took one of those little hand baskets, filled it, came back to the counter, and got another one. Quincy stood with a smile on his face shaking his head.

The manager looked a little nervous. He buzzed upstairs for the clerk to bring down another form. He looked at Quincy, who hunched his shoulders in the air, and continued to empty the baskets. By that time I returned with a third hand-basket. I thought I might as well get as many things as I could. My instructions were not to go over $100.00 dollars; so as long as I came in under that, it didn't matter how many items I got. Anyhow, if I went over, we had the finance to pay for it. I thought of everything I could, even a little gift to use for the stocking my husband would get.

I had spinning tops, yo-yos, checker board games, Candy Land, coloring books and crayons, princess crowns, plastic wands, marbles, little toy trucks, paper cut-out dolls, hand puppets, Ball and Jacks, and colorful modeling clay.

I continued to add things up in my head as I shopped, and the final tab at the register came to $83.00. I had gotten everything I needed, so there was no use pushing the dollar amount to the max. From the expression on the manager's face, I think he found it hard to believe I found as much as I did for that amount of money. Quincy signed the other form, and the sales clerk who brought the big box from the stockroom, helped us to the car with all the blessings. We went back into the store to thank the manager again, and Quincy asked if we could pray for him and the success of his business, and for blessings to fall on his life.

He was very receptive, saying that almost everyone the store had given to in the past said *'thank you'*, but we were the first ones to ever ask to pray for him and his business. He wished us a Merry Christmas, and said we could be sure that our church would be on their charity donation list for next year. We drove home almost in complete silence. We were amazed to see the hand of God at work this evening. Yes, we are in the season of celebrating the birthday of Christ as a baby however, we tend to forget that He is the reigning king who could do anything!

NINETEEN

With the new arrival on its way, I often thought about Lizzy. Subconsciously I must have, in some sort of way, disconnected myself with the stillborn baby I delivered, and replaced it with having Lizzy. She was the one I held in my arms the day of her birth. She had the precious little face, fingers, and toes that I kissed. She was the first life I held in my hands after the labor, and pains of delivery.

Now I was pregnant again. Thank God it's not like it was the first time. I am truly excited. I love Quincy so much. I can hardly wait to have our child. Quincy is so full of loving-kindness; I can't help but think that even if

I had not given Lizzy up, he still would have considered her to be ours.

When we were Christmas shopping for the give-a-way, I put several things in the basket for the infants and toddlers we have at the church. Most of the children of our congregation come from two parent households, but there are several who do not have a father in their life. One young lady lives with her parents, and I know of another who lives with her grandparents. Her name is Clairese. She has the toddler. Clairese was well aware that her sinful ways led her to the mistakes she made. She admitted to being rebellious, headstrong, and disobedient when living with her parents.

After her pregnancy, her parents said she had to leave from under their roof. She had no other relatives to stay with in Illinois, so she asked her grandparents if she could come and live with them. Quincy said when they came to him to ask his advice, all he could tell them to do at that time was to pray, and follow their heart. That was more than two years ago. From what I gather, they were not prepared to undertake such as burden. Anything like this would cause dishevel in the family, and drive a wedge between the grandparents, and their own children.

The next thing he knew, Clairese was living with her grandparents. She came to the altar and repented of her sin. Quincy said she joined the church, worked part-time during the day, and finished her high school courses at night. The grandparents were never over burdened with helping out with the baby while their granddaughter proved she was serious about changing her life. The parents finally came around to forgiving Clairese, and asked her to forgive them. Her grandparents said they were graced to be the medium while they all came to realize the truth of Romans 3:23... "For all have sinned, and come short of the glory of God".

Buying the little baby things brought a smile to my face, reminding me of what was soon to be announced. Still, it made me right melancholy at times, because they reminded me of the little things I brought for my Lizzy who left me not more than one year ago this month.

⸻

I sometimes thought about the young man, Robert Williams. But, I think my thoughts were much more about life, and the funny unexpected turns it puts you through. I thought about the many strange and dishearten things that can happen in someone's life. Yet, in the midst of it all, you never know that God is 'setting' you up for a miracle.

I've asked the Lord to allow me to think of the happiness the William's family must be having, now that they all are together again. I can only think that God has a plan for all of our lives. It's up to us to follow it. When things roll off the beaten path for us, it makes us wonder..."*Is this truly a part of God's plan. Or is it mine?*"

Then, I remember in His Word it says, He not only has a plan for our life, but thoughts too.

"For I know the thoughts that I think toward you, saith the Lord, thoughts of peace, and not of evil, to give you an expected end." (Jeremiah 29:11)

So, we have no reason to want someone else's life when the Lord has something especially designed for our own. That alone makes me feel good about my future. Anyway, to keep thinking about...*What if I had done this, or what if I had done that,* keeps you running back to the past when all of the good *stuff* in life is probably in front of you.

Memories of past things don't change and having fond memories is a good thing.

I'm working with the older children for the Cantata, but last year I was a single parent, and volunteered to work with the little tots, because my little girl was one of them. I wanted her to participate, but I was still a full time working mom. Lizzy was enrolled in the day care for four days a week and she had to be picked up by a certain time. Because of my schedule at the hospital, I could only pick her up two days a week. The other days fell on my Mother and Father.

For that reason, I thought it best for her not to be involved in the skit. She was my little angel; and I was sorry that she just couldn't be one in the Christmas play. I opted for her to say a short poem. We called them recitations.

For as long as I could remember, we've done this sort of thing in our churches. I ought to know, because I still remember one of the speeches I did when I was a child. Every parent beams with pride when his or her little child stands before the church and recites his Christmas, or Easter speech. And, they are so proud when their child comes through with flying colors, and takes their little bow, or curtsy. The parents and relatives applaud with thunder, as if their little tike had just recited the Gettysburg Address.

Well, not to be the *pot that called the kettle black*, I was one of those parents too. I remember every word Lizzy said, because I was the one who wrote her poem. As a matter of fact; I wrote all the speeches for the two to four year olds last year.

Lizzy's speech was entitled *"The Christmas Story"*.

The Christmas Story

**This is the Christmas story
Jesus was born in all His glory!**

When Pastor Folks invited me to his mother's house last year for Christmas, that night sitting on the sofa enjoying the flickering flame of the dancing fire; he told me that was one of the things he liked about me that got his attention.

I was surprised that he knew I was the one who wrote the speeches for that Sunday school class. I asked him how he knew I was the one responsible for doing it. He teased me saying:

"You'd be surprised how much a pastor knows about his members."

Then he admitted the head teacher for that class just happened to share the information with him, but said he would have guessed it anyway. So, I asked him how he could have done that, and he simply said;

"Because before you volunteered to help out with that class, that age group never had a part in the Christmas program."

We exchanged some more small talk. He shared some things, and then I shared some things. He made a comment, and then I said something to the effect that it doesn't get any better than this. I forget what we were talking about. But, the next thing I knew, he was down on one knee in front of me, asking me to be his wife. I was stunned beyond words, and didn't know what to say. That's when he came through with his *famous* statement, "say yes, say yes", so I did.

TWENTY

Snow was in the forecast for later today. Fortunately this Wednesday was my early off day. The temperature had dropped considerably since November, and I knew it was time to bring out the overcoat. The prediction was to expect a light snowfall accumulating to about two to three inches, but it wasn't supposed to start until four, or five o'clock. That's when the thermometer was really supposed to dip.

Quincy was awake, but he was still in the bed. He volunteered to take me to work, and to come back to pick me up if I thought the weather would catch me, but I told him no. That was alright. He was so protective. That's one of the things I loved about him. Anyway, I had such a short day; I didn't want it breaking into his day. I knew he was preparing a special teaching for Bible study this evening, and he probably needed that alone time. But, just in case the snow didn't hold off until after work, I reached in the closet, and got my boots.

The day went by quickly, and thank goodness; *no* snow. I called home before I left work to see if Quincy wanted me to pick up anything on the way in. Actually, I called because I was feeling a little melancholy, and wanted to hear the assurance of his voice. It had only been five hours since I left the house, and I was missing him all ready.

"Okay, I asked myself, what's wrong?"

He said the only thing he needed for me to bring home to him was *me*. *'Oh boy'*, I thought. I know I'm in trouble now. Both of our minds, or should I say...our bodies, were on the same wave link.

"Lord", I said, talking out loud, "This must be You, because I wasn't trying to go *there...at least not today."*

I know the Word says that God will give us the desires of our heart, and You sure must be reading my heart, because that's in my heart too, but I also envisioned this perfect setting for when I was going to announce the daddy thing.

Pastor Q and Donna

Man! If Pastor Q was at home waiting for me now, in the middle of the day, there is no way of camouflaging this rounding bulge forming across my mid-section. I knew I would stand a better chance of keeping my secret another week to ten days, or if our time of intimacy happened in the evening.

Rather than be selfish about what I wanted, and what my plans were, I had to put my husband's feeling before mine. I knew there were many women who wished they had the kind of husband I had. I know that to be true, because only four years ago, I was one of them. Still, after my own fall in life, I repented, and tried to remain faithful to God. Though I was in my early twenties, I chose to live vigilant before the Lord, and to watch my Christian walk. I had no idea that someone else was watching it too.

Quincy is a godly man, a called pastor/preacher, and a true romantic from his heart. Our first encounter with each other was pretty rocky, but he didn't let that deter him. I remember a few Sundays after that initial meeting I sat in church, but being overwhelmed with my own problems, my mind was somewhere else.

The service had ended, and I was still sitting in my seat. After greeting some of the parishioners, he came back up the aisle to see if I needed any assistance. He greeted me with a handshake. For some reason, at that instant my heart began to do flip-flops, which was uncanny, because as my pastor I shook hands with him many a time.

He had come to my aid a few times in the previous month, and I know it was a sacrifice on his part, but he said he didn't mind. It was his pleasure. Some other things occurred that caused us to meet up again, and that's when he asked if he could see me on a social level. I turned him down. I sure was not in the market to date a preacher; and the thought of going out with my *own* pastor was weird.

Nonetheless, on that Sunday when he held my hand in his, the whole time we were talking, I didn't even realize he was still holding my hand. It was when he asked me to go to dinner with him, that I went to pull my hand back, and he wouldn't let it go until I said 'yes' I'd go.

The compassion and warmth of his touch stayed with me all that day, and sometimes even to this very day, when I think about it, I can feel it. I don't know if there's any such thing as knowing the exact moment when love enters your heart, but for me (even though I denied it that day) it must have been the moment I felt the touch of his hand wrapped around mine.

There was something in his gentle touch that said, *'I'll protect you; your safe with me'*.

I pulled the car into the space at the back of the house, so I could come through the kitchen door. Knowing my husband like I did, he probably had some small romantic lunch prepared and waiting for me. He might even have one of our favorite love songs playing on the stereo in the living room.

Maybe it would be: "When A Man Loves A Woman", by Percy Sledge, or "Hello Stranger", by Barbara Lewis, or even "This Magic Moment", by The Drifters.

I could imagine him standing in the kitchen near the counter, or in the living room with his bathrobe on. He'd have a long stem red rose between his teeth. Then he would slowly move towards me, swaying back and forth to the music, and when he'd reach me, he would take me in his arms for a close up and *personal* slow dance.

Need I say more!

We would forget about eating lunch, and end up in our bedroom agreeing with each other for *Jeremiah 29:11.*

⁓

I stopped daydreaming, and took the keys out of the ignition. I locked the car, and fished on the key ring for the house key. Taking a deep breath, I turned the lock, and came through the door. I stood for a brief second to adjust my eyes from the cold.

Well, what do you know? There was a lunch (of sort) on the table, but it was for one. I didn't hear any music coming from the stereo. For that matter, I didn't hear anything at all. I sat my purse and keys on the counter, and moved into the living room. No Quincy. I began to feel a little let down, but I didn't give up hope. Maybe he's upstairs waiting. I called out, "honey, I'm home". No answer. I pulled the living room drapes to one side. I glimpsed out front. *'Umm that's funny',* I thought, *'His car is here.'* This time I went to the stairs, and called up.

"Honey, I'm back."

"Hey, I'm up here", he hollered back from the bedroom.

I sprang up the stairs, and swung open our bedroom door. Have you ever had the wind knocked out of you? Not like when you're playing football, or something like that, but a drizzling deflating wind, like when you let the air out of a balloon. Quincy was fully dressed, sitting on the bed, and tying the laces on his *Wing Tips'.*

"Hi babe, I thought I would have to leave you a note. Man! This could not have come at a worse time."

Quincy moved from the bed to the door where I was standing to give me a quick peck on the lips.

"What is it? What's happened?"

He saw the concerned look on my face.

"Oh, he said, nothing to worry about.

It's not any sort of an emergency or anything.
You know how Pastor Thomas has been trying to get together with us pastors about forming a 'Minister's Fellowship? Well he called about half an hour ago, and said he knew it was short notice, but they were going to meet over at 'Highway and Hedges Ministries'.
The meeting is at one O'clock, (he looked down at his watch). They want to try and draw up the proclamation for the alliance today, so they want as many of us who can make it, to be there."

He reached for Donna's hand, so she could follow him down the stairs.

"I fixed you a little something to eat. Did you see it?"

"Yes."

He opened the hallway closet door to pull out his long overcoat, scarf and hat.

"Oh, I don't know how long the meeting will be, but it'll probably last a couple of hours. So, instead of coming all the way back home, I'm gonna head over to the church. Remember? The Single's Ministry is coming in early before Bible study to separate and organize all the toys."

He picked up his briefcase, and gave me another kiss, and turning the doorknob said,

"So, I guess I'll see you tonight at Bible study. Bye."

I stood there in the middle of the living room floor wanting to cry. I couldn't believe what just happened. What was this…some kind of a test…some kind of joke, or something? With drooping shoulders, I made my way to the kitchen to get my lunch… and a small quiet voice reminded me—*my* desire was answered. I knew it was the Lord, but I had *two* desires, *two* requests. Now that this feeling had stirred up in me; it just couldn't be the end of it. It just couldn't!

TWENTY ONE

It hadn't been an hour since I prayed about not being selfish, and I was already beginning to regret it. I believe my husband was disappointed that our afternoon was spoiled too, but I couldn't help but think I was more disappointed than he. At least in my mind, I got the short end of the stick, but there I was again, being selfish.

I had such high expectations of this wonderful, romantic interlude; only to be out done by the *call* of the *collar*! A hunger pain brought me out of my musing, and I made my way to the kitchen to uncover the plate my husband made for my lunch. I could see he took care in making the sandwich. He had sliced some fresh fruit, and put it on the side of the plate. He had a cup and saucer and a selection of teas in the middle of the table, and the kettle was ready to be turned on. I didn't bother with heating the water. I just got a glass of milk from the refrigerator, and sat down to the kitchen table. I could feel the *'blues'* coming on. I knew if I let it overtake me, I would never show up for Bible study tonight, or for the rehearsal for the Cantata. It was scheduled for 5:00p and I couldn't disappoint those who were depending on me.

    After I showered, and took a short nap, I felt much better. There was still plenty of time left before I had to leave for the church, so I decided to have that cup of tea while I snacked on a few cookies. Aside from the craving for those big hamburgers, I was known to be a 'cookie monster'.

    Since it seemed like Quincy wouldn't have much chance to eat, unless he went by a fast-food place, I thought I'd bake a chicken. While that was baking, I boiled some potatoes and eggs. It wouldn't take long to make some potato salad, and put it in the 'fridge. I glanced around the decorated living room. It had come a long way from the few little trinkets we had a couple of weeks ago. It wasn't fully what I'd liked for it to be, but we were staying within a budget. We would add to what we had year-by-year. The one thing we did agree to get that might be kind of expensive was a wreath for the front door.

    Actually it wouldn't be an expense that was out of our budget because the Lord put so much money back in our pocket by giving us the toy blessing. Quincy said he would stop by one of those Nurseries sometime this week, and pick one up.

When I finished my lunch, I grabbed a magazine, and sat in the living room waiting for the chicken to bake, and the potatoes and eggs to boil. I began to hum a Christmas carol to myself. The songs made me think to turn the radio on. Surely one of the local stations would be playing Christmas music by now.

There were always the standards; "White Christmas', "The Christmas song: (Chestnuts Roasting on an Open Fire)", "What Child is this?" and "I heard the bells on Christmas Day".

Before I sat down, I went back to check on the chicken. The eggs were done, but the potatoes needed another ten minutes. Christmas music brings cheer to my spirit. I sang along with the radio, and flipped through the pages of the magazine. Then, the foiled plans of the day crept back into my mind. I guess some things happen for a specific reason, because the very next page I turned to, a big name store was advertising a product they had on sale for the holiday.
To indicate that this *hubby* knew what his wife wanted for Christmas, the ad featured an animated drawing. Underneath the picture were the words: "I saw Mommy Kissing Santa Clause". *Well that does it! I thought. Everybody's getting kissed but me!*

I hopped up from the sofa, and went to the stereo. I thought it would make me feel better if I put on a few records, and played some love songs just for me. I knew I would have to search through a stack of them to find the ones I wanted. I lifted the top on the console cabinet to find some 45rpm's stacked on the spindle. I pulled the arm back to lift them off.

I stopped to look at one of them. What in the world!

Quincy *was* planning an interesting afternoon for us.

I read the titles on the labels. I held every song I thought about on the way home, and some more I hadn't thought of. Oh my God! I looked at the clock on the kitchen wall. The chicken still had about a half hour to cook. I reshuffled the stack of 45's, and put "Hello Stranger" on the bottom, so it could be the first to drop down.

I had a brilliant idea rolling around in my head. I removed the pot of potatoes, poured the hot water off, and then fill the pot with cool tap water. I dashed up the stairs, and went into the bedroom. Who says Quincy has to do all the romancing? I'll just make a few plans of my own.

Donna reached way to the back of her closet feeling for the hanger that held her beautiful new negligee. She was saving it for later, but this was later enough for her.

She hung it on the back of the bathroom door. Next she ran the hot curlers through her hair, and pinned the locks up on her head in an Up-do. She didn't want her shoulder length hair distracting Quincy while he was preaching. Downstairs, she threw together the potato salad, and turned the oven off.

Pastor Q and Donna

On her way to the church she would stop in the grocery store. That way, she could kill two birds with one stone.

⸻

In the store she purchased a fragrant bottle of bubble bath, and a long stem red rose. The clerk put it in one of those little tube water holders, and wrapped foil around it for her. She had the note in her purse she had written to her husband before she left the house. Donna had dabbed it with a little of her expensive perfume, and left the lipstick imprint of her lips on the message inside above her 'I Love You' signature.

She planned to sneak back to Quincy's office just before the benediction, and put the envelope in his coat pocket. Donna wanted to be sure she left early enough to get a ten to fifteen minute start on her husband, because she had to get home, change her clothes, retouch her makeup, and run her husband's bath.

She was glad the rehearsals were right on point. Her husband's teaching was great. The auxiliaries were going to put the finishing touches on everything this coming Saturday.

When Donna got home she changed into her lace and silk negligee, and unpinned her hair. She poured half the bottle of foaming bubble bath in the tub and ran the water. She wanted to be sure the bubbles were thick and high. Next she added the fragrant body oil to the hot water, and the aroma filled the room. The bathroom was beginning to steam up, and she didn't want her hair to frizz. She left the bathroom, but left the door on a crack so the aroma would seep into the bedroom.

Donna got the small bag off the bed, and looked at the clock on the nightstand. She had to move fast. She lit three candles, and set them on saucers in the bathroom. Donna checked herself in the mirror on the dresser.

Thank goodness the pleated design of the empire waist hid any mid-section bulge that may have otherwise been visible. But once Quincy viewed the nylon and lace appliqué over her bosom, she was sure it would draw his attention upward.

Donna thought she heard Q's car come in the drive. She sprayed some perfume in the cleavage of her bosom, sprayed a peep in the air, and a squirt on the bed pillows. Grabbing the rose, she skirted half way down the steps, left it on the stairs, and ran to the stereo to press the *on* button.

Donna heard the key turn in the door. Her heart was pounding so hard, she felt like a school girl on her first date. She barely made it back to the steps. She placed the rose between her teeth, and struck a seductive pose.

Pastor Q came through the door just as the songstress was singing…"seems like a mighty long time, shoo wop de wop my baby ooh-ooh."

He dropped his briefcase on the floor, removed his coat and scarf and threw them on the chair. When he got a good look at what Donna was wearing, he said:

"You are a *dang-er-ous* woman!"

Donna removed the rose from between her teeth, and let her arm drop to her side. Her husband moved closer to the stairs.

"Oh, I see you got my note."

"Girl! Are you c-r-a-z-y? Suppose someone had gotten hold of that note?"

"*Someone* did. And I see he knew just where to find me."

She extended her arm, and touched his cheek with the rose. She let the bud move across his lips and down his neck to his chest. The music was still playing in the background. Quincy gently took the rose out of her hand, being careful of the thorns. Donna moved slowly down one step, and said,

"I've fixed you something to eat, but if you're not that hungry, we can—"

She leaned closer to him, and whispered something in his ear. A soft moan escaped through his lips.

"Mrs. Folks, you do realize that you are talking to a married man?"

"Yes Sir, I do. But, if this night isn't everything you expected... *and more*. Maybe you can take it up with my pastor."

Quincy was intoxicated; the perfume, the music, the provocative lingerie rent him powerless.

He was trembling when he took her in his arms, but the passion of his kiss told her everything she needed to know. As they turned to ascend the stairs, the next record dropped down from the spindle onto the turntable. Right on cue the singer hit his mark bellowing out, *"When A Man Loves A Woman"*.

It was magic!

TWENTY TWO

    Thursdays were Donna's off days, so she and the *Pastor* slept in. She didn't want to leave her bed, but it was a little after ten o'clock, and she felt a hungry twinge. If she remembered correctly it was after midnight when Quincy went downstairs to fix them a snack. He came back with a chicken leg and a thigh on one plate, and the wing and part of the breast on the other. He added a clump of potato salad on the side of each of their plates, and made some hot coco. He brought everything up on a serving try, and they dove right in. After two or three bites, they looked at each other and broke into laughter. They must have been hungrier than they thought!

Quincy got up to go to the bathroom, and Donna threw on her robe to go fix them something to eat. First, she went to her purse to get the supplements.

Downstairs, she heated some precooked sausage patties in the skillet, and then scrambled three eggs while she was waiting for the toast to pop up. She put the condiments on the carrying tray, and the cups for the instant coffee. Percolated would have been better, but she didn't want to wait until it dripped. All in all the breakfast preparation took about ten minutes.

When she came through the bedroom with the tray, Quincy scooted up to a higher sitting position. He had been leaning back, propped up on a couple of pillows with his hands resting behind his head. He started to get up to help her with the tray, but she told him to stay put. Donna liked seeing him lying there unstressed, and relaxed.

They lingered in the bed a while talking about the church, and what the rest of the year was going to look like. He told her the 'Clergy Alliance Fellowship' (that was the name they voted on), looked like it was going to be a very strong group. They formed a tentative board, and selected officers. That's when Quincy told her he was nominated to *chair* the committee for community events and annual fund raising. Although being 'Chair' at the present time meant, you were it! You were the committee. He said he told them he would let them know if he would take the position or not as soon as he discussed with his wife.

Releasing a slight chuckle, he said,

"I was going to tell you about it last night when I got home however; I got a little distracted when I came through the door."

They talked about the Christmas Cantata, and Pastor Folks told his wife again, how much he appreciated her. He said he believed her involvement in the programs at church, not only helped to encourage the parishioners, but helped to spear on church growth as well. He leaned over to give her shoulder a kiss.

"Not only that" he said, You have encouraged me to have hope again that the vision God gave me for the Ministry can come to fruition. I Love you Mrs. Donna, *'First Lady'* Folks."

"And, I love you too Pastor Quincy Folks, *'Mighty Man of God!"*

Those endearing words stirred his heart as well as his emotions. He knew he was blessed to have a wife like Donna; one who believed in him, and in what he was commissioned to do.

He had asked God for a wife he could trust with his heart, and with his ideas. If a man had enough love and trust from his wife, well…well, he was confident he could do almost anything!

Quincy understood that there was more than the physical side to a good relationship, and he sure had to pray that the arousal Donna stirred in him (at that moment) with her words…*'Mighty man of God',* would subside so he wouldn't appear to be too selfish.

The last thing they talked about was Donna's upcoming vacation time. Quincy told her he had already paid for the tickets, and made reservations to take her to the Amish Dinner theatre she wanted to go to. He also told her the outing was not one of her Christmas presents. It would be a yearly event for the both of them for as long as she wanted to go there.

During their talk, they jotted down people's name, and the things they wanted to pray about for them.

They kneeled down next to the Chaise lounge chair, and prayed. After prayer, Donna showered and dressed. It was well past the usual hour she visited with Sister Richardson. It's not like she had an appointed time to be there, but she knew Sister Richardson would be watching her clock in expectation.

Quincy called Pastor Thomas to let him know he would accept the position with the Fellowship. When he gave it some thought, he probable should have said *we* accept the position, because he knew he would need Donna's help with most of the planning.

Pastor Q and Donna

His mind turned to the message he was preparing for this Sunday. He worked on it in intervals, because of being preoccupied with other ministry matters. Now was the time to get back to it. For some reason he felt more inspired to complete what he had started. He had a good couple of hours to work on the message, and he prayed it would be, without interruption. Donna's visit with Sister Richardson would last for at least that long.

They planned to go shopping for the wreath for the front door when she got back home. His office at home was the extra bedroom across the hall from their bedroom. The house had three bedrooms, but the one at the end of the hall was what he called the official guest bedroom.

His mother or other family members stayed in that room when their visits required an overnight stay. His office was the smallest of the three, but it was adequate for what he needed. It had a small desk with chair, two bookshelves, a floor lamp, a telephone, and the recliner he moved from his bedroom when he married Donna. He still sat in it for occasional reading, or snoozing if he didn't want to lie down.

The message of hope sprang from his pen. He originally started the sermon going in another direction, but the inspiration in the text was now moving him toward something else. He was being inspired while he was writing the revelation that came to his mind. *Surely*, he thought... *if this is giving me hope for a new beginning in the New Year; it's bound to do the same for the congregation.*

Pastor Folks pondered over one of the statements in the message where he would ask a rhetorical question of the people. The question was: 'What would you have said if you were there the night of Jesus' birth? It's a baby boy! It's the Savior! It's the king!'

Isaiah chapter nine, verse six said this about Jesus:

"For unto us a child is born, to us a son is given, and the government shall be upon his shoulders. And he shall be called *Wonderful Counselor, Might God, Everlasting Father, Prince of Peace*".

He was thinking how we all need Jesus to be something different to us in each of our personal lives. We all need Him for one thing, yet at different intervals in our lives He's still the *One* who fits the bill. *The old folks said: "He's our all-in-all!"*

Time had dwindled down, and he knew Donna would be coming in soon. He folded his notebook, and went through the bedroom into the bathroom. He turned on the faucet to let the water run hot for his shave. After he shaved, he turned on the other faucet in the tub, and stepped into the shower. Instantly flashbacks of last night flooded his mind.

Though he tried to put it out of his mind, he couldn't help but think; *that is a bath I will remember for the rest of my life!*

Quincy looked for something casual to wear. Donna loved to see him in his Ban Lon shirts, but this wasn't Ban Lon weather. It was getting colder, and the forecast even called for a possibility of snow flurries. He hoped it would hold off until they finished shopping for the wreath.

Pastor Q and Donna

The gated area for the live trees and other fresh cut plants was on the outside of the nursery. Both he and Donna loved to smell the fragrance of a fresh cut Evergreen, and Pine trees. Since they decided not to purchase one this year, Donna found one of those room freshener sprays that was suppose to scent the air like a fresh cut Christmas tree. Needless to say, it didn't! It was just as artificial as those aluminum trees manufactures were making now days.

Donna enjoyed her visit. She told her husband that Sister Richardson's family was planning to pick her up on Monday so she could spend Christmas with them. She would be visiting with them through New Year's Day. Deacon and Sister Allen were taking good care of her every need, and she wanted to show her appreciation to them by buying them a Christmas gift.

Donna knew the few dollars she was given to purchase a gift wouldn't stretch very far, but she would be sure to get something nice, even if she had to chip in the difference. Quincy wanted to leave right away, so they skipped lunch, and grabbed an apple, and a tangerine from the bowl on the kitchen counter. Luckily Donna had eaten a bag of potato chips on the way home.

TWENTY THREE

They got the wreath, and went on to the department store to purchase the gift for the Allen's. Donna found a nice set of plush monogrammed bath towels. Not knowing what would coordinate with their bathroom, she chose the white towels. They were embroidered with a large cursive "A", in black lettering, and had gold tone fringe at both ends of the towels. She quickly added some choices of wrapping paper and tape to her gatherings, and they went to the checkout lanes. And boy, was it ever a line.

Quincy held her items as they inched along in the line. He was trying to think of another gift he would get for his wife, now that they agreed the Amish dinner theatre would be a yearly event to commemorate the first date they shared together.

Donna was like Quincy when it came to thinking about family and gift giving. They thought of family all year round. So, whenever they were out shopping for any reason, and they saw something that reminded them of a family member, or thought it was something that person would like, they purchased it. It could be something to give to them now, or something they would save for later. If anything came up like a graduation, a baby shower, or an anniversary, most of the time they had what they needed right there. And the best thing was; they didn't have to settle for a last minute something that said they didn't put any thought, or love in their giving.

The commotion of a little child in the next lane over begging for a particular toy brought Quincy out of his musing. The boy must have been about four, or five years old. Evidently he thought the little temper tantrum he was kicking up would get him the toy he wanted.

However, the gentleman who seemed to have been his father, took the toy away from him, and stuck it on one of the shelves near the register where they were standing. Then he leaned over, taking the little tike by the arm, and whispered something in his ear. Immediately the outburst stopped, and the boy's face straightened up. My lips pressed up in a grin. I don't know what his father promised him, but I can almost bet it wasn't the toy he put back on the shelf.

When we left the store a light dusting of snow was covering the ground. We didn't want to go anywhere fancy for dinner, or anywhere too far out of the area, not knowing what the weather would turn to, so we chose one of the local steak house restaurants on the main *drag*.
Quincy gave our names to the attendant at the counter, and was told it would be a ten to fifteen minute wait before we could be seated.
We didn't mind the wait.

We came in at the beginning of the dinner hour; a little after five o'clock. If we had come any later, we would have surely run into the real dinner crowd.
We sat in the waiting area, and enjoyed the Christmas music playing in the background. I sat admiring the decorations. We greeted the older couple sitting across from us, and the younger couple seated to our left. The older couple said it was their wedding anniversary. It was very noticeable that the young couple to our left was expecting a baby.
Quincy asked if this was their first, and she said no. They had a two-year old toddler at home being watched by his aunty. The husband said his wife was due the first week in January, if she held out that long, and they wanted to have one more dinner date before the holiday, or the baby, whichever came first. He said if the doctors were right, they might even have a New Year's baby. We all had a little chuckle when he patted his wife's tummy.

Somehow I knew we would not escape the conversation without *the inevitable question* being asked. Sure enough the older couple obliged us.

"No", Quincy said. "We don't have any children yet." Then, taking my hand in his, he continued, "We are coming up on our first year anniversary in February, so who knows?"

That sounded like a hopeful *who knows* to me. Before anyone could respond, the maître d' called the older couple's name, and they followed him out, wishing everyone a 'Merry Christmas'.

Donna had to think of something to divert the conversations from turning back to babies. She felt awful. Donna loved her husband so much, but she was so close to his Christmas surprise, she didn't want anything to spoil it.

During the course of the meal Quincy's thoughts floated back and forth on the events of the evening before. He smiled every now and then, and Donna asked him what on earth he was smiling about.

He just said, "Oh, nothing in particular."

They were seated in a booth near the window. The snow was still light, but falling at a more steady pace. Donna commented on how *'Christmassy'* it made everything look, but she hoped they didn't get too much of it. She had one more day of work before her vacation started, and she wanted to be able to make it in. Quincy told her not to worry about that. He would drive her to work, and pick her up if she wanted him to.

At times they would let the conversation drop, and just listen to the muffled sounds of voices, and the tinkling of glasses and silverware in the background.
People were coming and going. They had finished their meal, but sat there awhile enjoying each other's company. Quincy caught the waiter's attention to ask for the check. Luckily he was facing towards the front of the restaurant, and could see him serving others.

Donna was seated across from him, and could see people as they were being seated beyond the both of them. She could also see when they were leaving out. Donna happened to looked up just as a Caucasian couple was heading out. They had to pass their table, and Donna made it a habit to smile a greeting at people who were passing by their table. The couple neared the table, and a gasp escaped her lips. When she raised her hand to her throat, she dropped her fork.
The passer by picked it up unconscious of who she was until he placed it back on the table and their eyes met. He was completely thrown of guard and stood looking at her. A tongue-tied 'Hello' stammered from his lips, and then he moved quickly away. Quincy felt the hair on the back of his neck stand up.

"What in the world was that all about? Who was the guy?"

Donna found her voice.

"That is a man I haven't seen for the past five years. His name is Derek."

Quincy reached across the table to take Donna's hand in his. He sensed this meeting was completely accidental. He was very familiar with the name, because Donna shared everything with him about her past before they were married.

However, Quincy knew something about this Derek that Donna didn't know. But, he knew he was not to share with her what happed a few months back concerning Derek, and Ron. Some things had to stay as they were until the Lord said it was time for them to be released; that is… if they were ever to be released.

His job now was to protect his wife, and to console her in whatever way he could when they got back home.

TWENTY FOUR

Donna decided to let *'sleeping dogs lie'*.

She had to use up her vacation time for the year no matter what she decided to do about the baby.

Her unit was having their Christmas party on Saturday December 19th.

With Sunday being such a full day at church for the both of them, she was not sure Quincy would want to go with her. It wasn't going to be one of those fancy things, because most of the staff was on duty that day. But, she should have known Quincy was always ready to support her in whatever she wanted to do.

Her unit scheduled the use of the conference room on their floor from 10:00a to 2:00p. Everyone was supposed to bring a dish to pass, and those who wanted to exchange gifts were free to do so; it was strictly up to them.

During that time people who were not scheduled to work on that day could come by and stay for as long as they wanted. The ones who were on duty would float in and out as time permitted. It was more for the fellowship than anything else because some of the day staff didn't know workers on the night staff, and visa versa.

Chairs were pulled away from the long table, and lined against the walls. I didn't want to take the chance on missing anyone, because I sometimes worked both shifts and know just about all the staff. Quincy walked me down to the employee's locker room so I could put my Christmas greeting in each cubby.

On the way back to the conference room, I decided to swing by my office. I wanted to be sure I brought home everything I needed while I was going to be out. Administration shifted a few supervisors from normal shifts to swing shifts to make sure the unit would be covered while I was out. That's another reason I had to let them know what I planned to do. If I was not going to stay, we would either have to go through the training process (which would be left up to me), or the hiring process; which would be on them.

We took the elevator back up to my office. I opened the door, and while I was flipping on the switch, I felt something under my foot. I froze in my tracks. Quincy was coming through the door in back of me and bumped into my back when I stopped. Slightly inside the door he must have stepped on the items too. I felt my stomach twinge, and my hands turned cold.

He bent down to gather the envelopes from the floor. He looked in my face, and saw the anxiety. Without even a hint of concern, he calmly said:

> "Look sweetie. Some of the staff put their greeting cards under your door. Maybe they thought they would not get a chance to see you today. Good thing you decided to come back to your office."

I was surprised the secret admirer episode was still in the back of my mind; after all, Quincy took care of everything and he never said it was anything more than some guy who thought he could get my attention. I don't know why I let it affect me the way it did.

Pastor Folks knew what the real deal was, so as a precaution he opened each card saying who it was from, and then handed it to his wife.

In her *'single'* days, Donna would have had a little gift, or trinket for everybody in the unit, but today the card and attached candy cane would have to do. The robe she got for Quincy was costly, and she made up the difference for Sister Richardson's gift to the Allen's. She didn't mind that because in a way, they were a blessing to her too.

There was also the financial token of appreciation Quincy was giving to the volunteer staff. She also didn't want to use into the money she needed to pay the seamstress for sewing the bars on her husband's robe. She could have had the company to do it when she ordered the robe, but she wanted a particular red cord to outline each bar.

Pastor Folks and Donna got up early for prayer on Sunday. While he shaved and showered, Donna pulled together some eggs, scrapple, toast, and coffee. They arrived at the church about twenty minutes before nine to find everything in order. The sidewalks from the curb to the church entrance had been cleared of snow; also the walkway leading from the small parking lot had been cleared.
There even was a path scooped out that came from the pastor's parking space to the back door of the church.

Inside, the church was warm and inviting. Pastor Folks smiled to himself thanking the Lord for such devoted parishioners as the deacons and the church custodian. Donna put her things up, and hurried out the door saying she would be back for prayer before morning service began. She crossed the sanctuary to the small hallway on the other side of the church where the Sunday school classrooms were located.
The teachers were in place and waiting as parents and their children staggered in. Mothers fussed with their little girl's dresses and bows, and a few of them moistened the end of their hankies with spit to wipe the chalky corners of their little boy's mouths.

Pastor Q and Donna

The Sunday school teachers entered the sanctuary trailed by their little tikes. The class sat in the place reserved for them on the front pew. The parents and grandparents got as close to the front as possible.

No matter how much a parent practices with his or her child at home, inevitably there are one or two children who will suffer from stage fright. Then, the parent has to come up front to stand beside him. Sometimes it works, and sometimes it doesn't.

⸻

Pastor Folks preached an inspiring message. Christmas services always had invited guest, and out of town family members. For that reason Pastor Folks didn't let an opportunity go by where he would not offer the call to salvation, and discipleship. When the call went out, two souls came forward to join the church, and we rejoiced with those whose names would be added to *'The Lambs Book of Life'*.

There would not be an official sermon at the Cantata this evening. The mixture of scripture, song, and reenactments were the message of the Christmas story. There was an air of excitement about the day, and this evening would be the culmination of a lot of hard work and practice.

After service, the men began to rearrange the front pews to make room for the scenery. The women brought in the costumes and put them in the classrooms that were assigned for the girls, the boys, and the adults that were in the play. Since we had to be back to church by 3:00 o'clock, some parents packed a lunch ahead of time for their family so they could stay through the day.

Quincy kept the Christmas stockings in the trunk of his car. We turned in the toys, but we held back the stockings as a surprise.

When the time drew near for the Cantata that evening, the parents assigned to assist the teachers went to their individual classrooms. I believe they were just as excited as the children. I know I was. They were all ready and waiting well before time.

The sanctuary lights were dimmed, and a voice began to read from the book of Luke, chapter two. The choir followed with the annunciation song: *'Joy To The World'*. We appreciated the way the choir director arranged each song to parallel with scripture readings, and dramatic reenactments that surround the birth of Christ.

Parents moved in and out of position with their Polaroid cameras to get a good snap shot of their child. It did cause a little distraction, but that's to be expected. Just before the Cantata ended Pastor Folks sent two high school boys to his car to get the big box out of the trunk.

A soloist from the choir sang *'O Holy Night'*, and then all the children came up front to sing *'We Wish You A Merry Christmas'*.

We made sure we applauded everyone who participated in the day's activities. We recognized every committee member, and every effort from each person from the pew to the back door. The congregation was asked to be seated for the toy give-a-way. Pastor folks asked the parents to help in reassuring that the Christmas packages were not opened in the sanctuary, and if everyone would remain seated, a special Merry Christmas gift from the pastor and 'First Lady' would be given to everyone in the building.

The ushers directed the congregation around pew by pew, and we handed a stocking to all who came. Pastor Folks wanted to be sure everyone in the building was served because he still had stockings available. Two young men urged on by the parishioner sitting next to them moved out into the aisle, and a Caucasian couple from way in the back came out behind them.

We always welcomed visitors, and wanted them to feel at home. They may, or may not have had anywhere else to go, but we wanted them to know they were a part of our family too. The two men said they stayed at the 'Y', and were invited by a member who donated some coats there this past week.

An eerie feeling came over Donna as the men moved away, and the couple standing behind them was next in line.
She managed to keep a fixed smile on her face, but her mind could not allow her to rationalize who she was seeing. *"Man"*, Pastor Quincy thought, *that guy looks familiar. I know I've seen him before.* He turned towards his wife, and seeing her face, he placed his arm around the back of her waist for moral support. She didn't move. Quincy reached for her hand. He knew God had ordained a special visitation for his wife.

"Hullo" the young lady said.

"Hello Pastor Folks" Robert said, extending his hand. Rachel and I thought we'd give you a nice Christmas surprise."

Pastor Folks found his voice. He gave them each a stocking, and a hardy handshake. He asked if they could stay a few more minutes until he finished up with what he was doing.

"Sure, Rachel's brought a little something for you too".

Pastor Folks nodded his head indicating to Mrs. Daily to come up to receive instructions from him. He asked if she would walk the visitors and Mrs. Folks back to his office, and he would join them as soon as had given the benediction, and dismissed everyone to the fellowship hall for refreshments.

In the office Rachel told Donna they had come alone. They thought it best for the children because they were making such good progress in adjusting to their new family. Robert and Rachel felt that any little change at this juncture might cause setbacks. Of course Donna understood.

Pastor Folks came through the door and shook Robert's hand again. He patted him on the back saying how happy he was to see him. Robert assured them that all was going well with his health, and with their family reunion. He told Pastor Folks he wanted to keep the promise he made to him when he was in the hospital; that he would stop by the church if he was ever in the area.

Rachel had a special Christmas gift to give to Donna. She reached in her purse and took out a brightly colored envelope. Donna opened the greeting card, and inside was a photo of two beautiful children. The girl was wearing a red winter coat with a matching hat, and the boy had deep brown wavy hair. His eyes were brown and his face was so much like his father's.

Mrs. Daily brought in some refreshments on a tray and placed them on the desk. Rachel was pleased to see that some hot cinnamon tea was on the tray with the cookies and other goodies. Robert said the kids were with Mr. and Mrs. McAfee. They often visited with the elderly couple. The McAfee's were like a second set of grandparents to their children. He said he and Rachel couldn't stay long. They only popped in for a short visit. After they left the church they were going to swing around to pick up the kids, and the whole family was going back to Walnut Creek to spend Christmas with all the other grandparents and family.

TWENTY FIVE

Donna lay in bed trying to relax. It was impossible to even think about going to sleep. Too many emotions impounded her mind. The happenings they had planned for that day were incredible enough, but to be outdone by the plans of God put the icing on the cake.

A visit from Rachel and Robert was completely unexpected. That was something that never entered her mind. NEVER!

She turned to look at the photo clipped to the greeting card on her nightstand. This was so amazing! Donna lay awake staring at the ceiling while memories and images drifted through her head.

The Rachel she met tonight was no longer the naïve little Amish girl she met in the hospital some three years ago.

The couple couldn't stay long, but Quincy insisted they go out for dinner, or at least for a cup of coffee. We ended up at a twenty-four hour pancake house that wasn't far from the church. We respected their wish to get back on the road, and chose a place that would give them easy access back to the main highway. Even though they used a road map to find where we were it was dark now, and more challenging to navigate their way back to the Interstate.

We settled for coffee and *more* dessert. In the short conversation that followed, Robert and Rachel shared some of the struggles they've come through. Neither of them seemed to have been disheartened about it, but praised God for the victories He's brought them through.

Robert confessed that when Pastor Folks and I visited him in the hospital that day, he thought we were already husband and wife. It wasn't until he inquired through the hospital's regular Chaplin that he found out Pastor Quincy was a single man. The Chaplin told him, he knew for sure I was not married.

Robert told Quincy he remembers the thought running through his mind: *'that's a shame. They would make such a wonderful married couple.'*

We exchanged telephone numbers and mailing addresses, and promised to stay in touch every few months of so. We knew we weren't *'family-family'*, but we had to admit there was a kindred spirit between us. As a friendly jester, and to make it easier on them, Quincy volunteered to lead them out to the Interstate with our car. It was a wonderful idea. When we got to where they were to exit onto the ramp, Quincy blinked his lights, and tooted his horn, and off they went into the night.

Donna was sure that once she told Quincy of his unexpected fatherhood, it would be one of the very first things he would share with Robert. Somehow Donna could sense the unspoken question lurking in the back of Rachel's mind. *"Will they have a wee one of their own?"*

The visit from Robert and Rachel was so unexpected, but God's timing is perfect. Donna was happy they had something to send along with them for the children. If it had been any other time, she would not have had ready-made gifts to put in their hands. This made her feel good. The twins would have a Christmas stocking filled with candy, toys, and most of all…Donna's love. They would not know who sent the gift, but their parents said they'd be sure to let the twins know that it came from special friends who loved them very much.

Rachel told Donna this was another event she would write in her diary. That it was a *special* lady who started her to keeping a journal about a year ago, and she's been doing it ever since.

Pastor Folks was looking forward to the whole week off. It was announced again during the morning and afternoon services that there would be no Bible study on this coming Wednesday night, December 23rd. The Pastor and Sister Folks' prayer was that everyone should have a safe and joyous holiday, and that they would enjoy their time with family and friends.

Donna was excited about their dinner theatre date. It was to be on tomorrow. However, for today she was going over to her folk's house to make Christmas cookies. Some of the cookies would be for the household, but most of them were for the neighbors. That was something her mother did every year.

Besides; spending this time together would give them a chance to have a nice mother/daughter talk. Both of her parents were at church last evening, but just in case they did not get a good look at the last couple who came up last night, Donna wanted to tell them who they were. Plus, she had a bit of news of her own she wanted to share with them.

Donna brought the photo of the twins along with her. She wasn't quite sure how her parents would react when they saw the picture of Lizzy. She just had to wait and see.

They both were happy to know who the visitors were. Mrs. Vaughn didn't recognize Rachel. After all, it had been the better part of three years since that day of the exchange, and even then she only got a glance of the young Amish girl when the nurse wheeled Donna over to her room. She remembered standing in the corridor peeking through the half opened door. The poor little girl looked so frail, so frightened; so unlike the lady she saw at church last evening.

The photo brought on a stint of mixed emotions from her parents. They had been such a major part of Lizzy's life from day one of her arrival until the day I took her back to her natural parents. It was a very moving moment for them.

With all that was going on, Donna thought this would be a good time to announce her own pregnancy. Her parents clapped their hands, hugged her several times, and kept saying:

"Hallelujah! Thank you Jesus!"

Donna knew they were excited for her, and for Pastor Quincy, but she swore the both of them to secrecy. She let them know that her husband didn't know yet, and she wasn't sure if she was going to tell him tomorrow night on their date, or if she could hold out 'till Christmas.

Now, with his mother knowing the news, and her parents knowing too, Donna felt a little guilty that Quincy would be the last to know. Furthermore, if they were having dinner at her folk's house Christmas Eve night, she didn't want to put any undue pressure on them. Maybe she'd better tell him tomorrow night. She could only imagine her parent's actions, and what their faces would look like trying to hold in the precious secret from their *Pastor!*

Donna's snack weakness has always been cookies, and today she was in the right place at the right time. She and her mother must have baked ten different varieties of delicious cookies. Donna sampled every one of them, sometimes twice. She also took a tin of cookies home for the household. Quincy was known to have a sweet tooth every now and then too.

When she let herself in, she saw where her husband had left a note for her on the kitchen counter. It said he would be right back. He went to pick something up for tomorrow's date night.

Now she was curious. What could he need for our date night?

Oh well, she thought. This will give me enough time to wrap my surprise gift for him. Donna went to get the gift from its hiding place. She made sure the small box was stuffed and padded with tissue paper so the item inside would not move about just in case Quincy decided to shake the box first. Sometimes he did that before he opened a present. Donna wrapped the box in beautiful shiny paper, and put a blue press-bow on top.

"Now", she said, "for the finishing touch."

She got one of her blank *Thank You* note cards from the desk drawer to write her husband a message. She put everything in her purse, and then went downstairs to prepare dinner.

Pastor Q and Donna

It was at the last minute when Quincy decided to go back to the jewelers to get the unique necklace he saw a few days ago. He hoped it was still there.

He had completed his Christmas shopping for Donna, his mother, and for the Vaughns. He was very pleased that he and Donna were able to present the Christmas love offerings to the volunteer staff at the church.

If it weren't for Donna helping with finances, he just couldn't see how they would be able to do the things they were doing. He knew in his heart he wanted to be able to do certain things, but it took a good wife to help figure it out. And not just with finances, but in other things too. He was blessed!

Yes. The locket was still there.

The locket was hanging from an eighteen inch sterling silver chain. And the locket itself was a little sterling silver bible that opened. It had the words HOLY BILBE on the front stamped in 14k gold, and under the words was a cross also embossed in 14k gold. The whole charm was only about a half inch square. The sterling silver leaflets opened to reveal Romans 8:28. Pastor Folks stood in the jewelers thinking on how pleased and surprised he was when the trustee board had decided to give him a Christmas bonus too. If it had not been for that, he most likely would not have been able to get this extra trinket. But, God knows your heart, and He answers your desires.

Lucy Heath

It wasn't that it was such an expensive gift...it's just that it was her...it was Donna. It was her strength. It was what she believed. It was what he believed for her. The jeweler said for a few more dollars he could have it engraved. Quincy went for it, and chose the three most powerful words he knew!

TWENTY SIX

Quincy reserved the five o' clock seating for dinner with the play starting at seven. He thought Donna looked like a beautiful little snow bunny. It was the way the faux fur on the hood of her white swing coat encircled her face. She didn't wear the coat often, but when she did, she looked stunning. She wore her red leather boots, and carried a matching purse.

Quincy was so excited. He had the jewelry box in the top inside pocket of his suit jacket.

He was glad the restaurant wasn't overly crowded. Their meal came quickly, and it was great food. Pastor Folks couldn't keep his eyes off of his wife.

At times he felt their conversation was a bit of a strain, but chalked it up to his own nervousness. It almost felt like it did when they came here on their first date.

He had to smile to himself every time he thought about the way he tricked Donna into going out with him on that Sunday. Well maybe *tricked* isn't the proper Christian word to use, but any way he knew it was time for him to start seeing her on a social level. He also remembers he didn't know what he would have done if she said 'no', because he had already purchased the tickets. All he could think of when he purchased the tickets was: *'If this ain't the Holy Ghost, I'm in big trouble'!* He hung in there and held her hand until she said 'yes', but he was *sweating bullets*.

Donna fiddled several times with the food on her plate trying to figure out when the best moment would be for her to present the gift to her husband. The Waiter came to clear the table, and brought two chocolate dinner mints on a serving saucer along with the bill. He served them a fresh round of coffee, and bid them an enjoyable evening.

"Honey!"

Quincy and Donna laughed out loud, because they both said honey at the same time. Donna reached in her purse, and brought out her gift just as her husband reached in his pocket to bring out his.

They laughed again.

"Looks like we both were thinking of the same thing", Donna said.

"Well. You know what they say", he replied. "Great minds think alike!"

"Honey, I'm so excited", Donna said, "let me go first."

"Okay, he said, Ladies first."

Donna handed the package across the table and asked him to read the card. Quincy was reading it silently, and Donna said,

"No. No, read it out loud."

He looked at his wife arching one eyebrow higher than the other, and gave her a sexy smile.

"You look so alluring tonight; your wish is my command."

"Just read the card! It's not what you think. You always think everything is about *that*."

Quincy cleared his throat and began to read:

> My Darling husband lets ring in the season
> And start this chapter anew
> Because this only begins to show the love
> I'll always have for you

Quincy picked up the box and shook it. It didn't make any sound.

"Quincy, just open the box."

He unwrapped the box, and the item inside was wrapped in more paper. At first glance it looked like a Christmas bell. He didn't get it! Donna told him there was more to the gift. It was a package deal, but first he had to read the second note. It was on the reverse side of the card.

> What's In A Name
> Quincy, Daniel, Westly, Shane
> Donna, Lucy, Grace, or Lady...
> What would you name a brand new Baby?

He wasn't sure if he was thinking the right thing or not. He didn't want to get his wires crossed up. Donna could see the confused look on his face, so she said:

Pastor Q and Donna

"Keep going. There's more."

He realized the funny looking bell was a baby rattle. Quincy reached in the box again and lifted up a piece of tissue paper, and saw what appeared to be a folded white handkerchief.

"Unfold it Pastor."

Quincy unfolded the little white fabric. It was an infant's undershirt. He held it up in the air with both hands, and read the words **Hello Daddy** printed in big bold red letters. For the first time in his life Quincy Folks was speechless!

His hands began to tremble. Quincy looked in his wife's eyes with all the love that he could exude from his being. He rose slowly from his seat, and moved in a daze towards Donna. Without thinking of where he was, or who was watching, he urged his wife to stand by gently lifting her hand. He took Donna in his arms. Tears filled his eyes, and he whispered in her ear,

"Thank you, thank you."

"No, Donna said, thank you."

Quincy was in a world of his own. When he came to himself, he remembered he was standing in the middle of a restaurant floor. He dropped his embrace. He felt slightly self-conscious. Then without giving it a second thought, he blurted out;

"We're having a baby. I mean my wife is going to have a baby. I'm going to be a daddy!"

The restaurant erupted in cheers and applauds. There was a round of Hip-Hip- Hooray coming from some of the men, and the patrons began clinging on their water glasses with their spoons. Quincy was only too happy to oblige. He took his wife in his arms and kissed her again. This time Donna was a little embarrassed!

They sat down and Quincy looked at the little baby things again. He did that two or three times shaking his head back and forth, moaning...um, um, um. He wangled his handkerchief from the back pocket of his pants, and wiped his eyes. His heart was pounding so hard in his chest. He was overwhelmed.

All was quiet except for the moving about of the attendants preparing the area for the theatrical presentation of the evening. Donna broke away from her own silence and pointing to the box on the table said,

"I take it that pretty little box on the table is for me."

Quincy was so overcome with Donna's news he completely forgot to give his present to her. He took his index finger, and slid the box across the table closer to his wife. Donna opened the box, and her heart melted.

Her eyes fell on the beautiful necklace. It was so exquisite, so precious. It was almost as if Quincy had anticipated the news she was going to give him for his Christmas surprise, and wanted to say thank you. She knew that couldn't have been so, because of his reaction. Still, if it were true, there was no greater words he could have said than those engraved on the back of the Bible pendant. **I Love You.**

They sat enjoying the Christmas play like true lovers who had met for the first time. Quincy held Donna's hand in his and every now and then he would give it a gentle squeeze, or she would think of how much she loved him, and would give his hand a loving caress. The sensual touch of her caresses sent electricity surging through his entire body.

Of course his mind tried not to go *there*, but he couldn't help it. Sure, he was a pastor, but he also (as they say) was *free*, *black*, and *willing*! He adored his wife, and now that both of their schedules were going to be relaxed for several days, he wanted to enjoy her.

All of a sudden the question of having an intimate encounter with Donna entered his mind. Not for selfish reasons. He wondered if it was proper, now that she was expecting. *Was it permissible? When do you stop intimacy? Will it hurt the baby?* He felt kind of silly. He didn't know the answers to any of these questions. He didn't even know who to ask.

'Actually', Quincy thought to himself, *'right now I'm too excited. I'm in love, and I'm confused. I can't even concentrate on the play. Everything is fogging together in my head. I don't know what's happening on stage…I only know what's happening in my heart.'*

TWENTY SEVEN

Quincy was so ecstatic and dazed, that for a minute I thought I would have to drive us home. I could already see from the attention I was receiving, I would have to calm him down.

He paced, he sat. He hugged me. He felt my stomach, and then he'd do it all over again. He didn't know what to do with himself. He wanted to call the folks, but it was after eleven o'clock, and I knew they would be in bed. I didn't want to put a damper on his excitement, so I found a tactful way of telling him they already knew. I told him his mother right out guessed it, and at Thanksgiving, my Mom was mighty suspicious. He said he felt badly, because he hadn't noticed.

I reassured him that was nothing to feel ashamed about. Most wives have to announce the happy occasion to their husbands anyway. And, as for our folks, I told him that as a rule of thumb, Mothers and Mother-in-laws are constantly on the lookout for signs of pregnancy. They can almost smell a baby on the way. They've probably been expecting to hear the news ever since the honeymoon night! Quincy laughed, realizing that Donna was telling the truth.

Instead of just kneeling together for their evening prayers, Pastor Folks thought he was being led by the Spirit to include their unborn child in family prayer with them. Of course the baby would always be included in prayer, but he was getting a vision of encircling Donna and the baby tonight as a symbol of provider and protector. He just had to see how he was going to do it.

He explained to Donna what he wanted to do, because if he wasn't careful and if he was not being led by the Spirit; it might seem a bit worldly, and sensual.

Donna got the idea of what he was trying to do, and in a jokingly way said she would try to *contain* herself. They both laughed.

Pastor Q and Donna

Pastor Q sat on the Chaise lounge because he had to be behind her in order to encircle her. Most times they knelt together at the side of the bed, or in front of the Chaise on their knees, but that still wouldn't work. He didn't like the idea of being on the floor.

Donna sat on the lounge in front of her husband. Pastor Q wrapped his arms around his wife's midsection, and folded his hands in a prayer clasp across her belly. This prayer was for their personal lives, and the favor of God for generational blessings through His Seed, and for the Lord's Will and destiny to be fulfilled in the life of their child, and their children's, children.

And right on cue, as if it was a sanction to the prayer, Quincy felt Donna's stomach move against his hands. The movement surprised her too. She said up until this time all she felt was little fluttering's, but this the first strong movement that had occurred.

They ended up praying for the church, and the body of Christ at large.

Wednesday was the day before Christmas Eve. Thank goodness there was nothing to do that would drag either one of us out of the house. We knew the streets and stores would be bustling with last minute Christmas shoppers. I couldn't help but think that most of them had lost the true meaning of the holiday due to commercialism. The reason we celebrate the season is because of Christ. Maybe I'm old fashioned, but I don't think so.

The stores were replacing the words **'Merry Christmas'** with *'Happy Holiday,* and *Seasons Greetings.'*

They say it's because they wanted to be more inclusive. But, inclusive of whom? I even saw one sign that said *'Merry X-mas.'* I don't know what that was all about. I didn't see other groups changing their wording from *'Happy Hanukkah'* to 'Happy Holiday'. Of course I know that the real reason was to take the name of *'Christ'* out of Christmas, so it could be a more secular celebration. But so far as I'm concerned, Christ was born for all, and He died for all. I guess that just about makes the celebration inclusive of everyone the way it is now... with Christ in the name!

I had to go out, but not to the department stores. I had to take the extra-large gift box over to the seamstress' house. She had finished with the *Doctorate* bars a couple of days ago, and I had to get Quincy's robe wrapped before I brought it home. I brought the silver foil wrapping paper with me. I decorated the box with a huge wired-rimmed red ribbon, and tied it off in a bow. I attached a card. I guess one could tell that cards and notes are my thing. I took the package to the car, and placed it in the trunk. Then I was on my way back home.

⸻

We left for my parent's house early Christmas Eve morning. We wanted to spend as much time with them as we could.

I'm a person who thinks of practical gifts that people can really use, but I also want the present to compliment who they are as a person. Along with the gifts we had for my folks, I also had the photo of Lizzy and her brother. I had taken it to the photo copy store to get it enlarged. I purchased a beautiful 8x10 frame to put it in.

Now we opened our gifts with my parents on Christmas Eve, since we would spend Christmas Day with Quincy's mother and family. However, I asked my folks not to open the last gift I gave them until Christmas morning. It was the picture of the twins. I wanted them to share that moment alone with each other.

Our original plan was to leave from my folk's house and head out for Wilmington. We were enjoying ourselves so much, that we let the time get away from us. Quincy thought a good nights rest might be in order since it was so late. That way we could head out early in the morning. We both knew that Christmas was going to be a long (but joyous) day, just like this one was. So, home we went. We were loaded down with Christmas goodies, plastic containers of leftovers, and a bag full of presents.

Quincy brought in the things we were going to keep at the house, and I told him to be sure he left the other tin of cookies in the car. It was my mother's gift to Sister Folks.

TWENTY EIGHT

It had only been two days since Donna had told Quincy the exciting news of the baby, and he couldn't stop looking at her. She was nearly four months pregnant, and he actually felt the baby move in his hands... his baby...their baby.

Maybe she was right, *he thought,* in waiting to tell me. It's only been a couple of days, and I must have asked her *'twenty times'* if she was all right.

Now that Quincy knew about the baby, Donna didn't have to conceal her daily vitamins and supplements, nor her visits to the doctor.

Donna looked in the mirror at the necklace her husband had given her. She thought how loving and caring he was, and what a wonderful father he would be.

Quincy repacked their small suitcases to accommodate their change of plans. Donna wished they could make their visit longer than one overnight stay, but they were already using one of those nights tonight here at home. They had to be back on Saturday evening to prepare for church on Sunday. It was a silly thing to think of that popped into her mind at that moment, and a flush of embarrassment came over her face.

She was just about ready to put her hair up in rollers, and her mind went back to Tuesday night when she sat huddled in her husband's embrace while he prayed for her and the baby.

His arms were strong and muscular, and his chest pressed against her back caused her to flinch. It was an awful thing to think about in *that* way because it was meant to be a sacred moment, *not one of intimacy*. But, she thought…*it is what it is!*

They had been so busy all the week they had let that part of their relationship go. She was use to Quincy coming up behind her; kissing the nap of her neck, or either he would walk up to her swaying to imaginary music extending his hand for a slow dance. The man had a saunter that wouldn't quit, even when he was just *plain* old walking!

When she thought about being at his mother's house for two more days; then the drive home, and church the next day too...Donna put the hair roller back in the plastic tub container.

She brushed through her hair, and let it fall down around her shoulders. She quickly freshened up at the sink, and dabbed some perfume in back of her ear lobes. Her favorite lipstick was in her purse, so the one on the counter would have to do.

Quincy was sitting on the bed waiting for his turn to get in the bathroom. When the door opened, Donna emerged. She held up her index finger and beckoned him to come to her.

> "Pastor Q, I know you're feeling a might tired (her voice was low and seductive), but I *do* believe I'm in *desperate* need of prayer."

Quincy's eyes shifted from side to side in a questioning look. Then, all of a sudden he got her drift. A smile broadened on his face. He rose from the bed to approach her at the bathroom door. Donna continued to perform.

> "Now, if I were you. I'd quickly brush my teeth, and *not* slip into something more comfortable."

She gave her lips a pucker.

> "I'll be waiting for you over there on the Chaise. (Donna pointed across the room) And, *Oh yes*; I would like to begin with that *very* imaginative

'*New*' family prayer embrace you came up with the other night."

Pastor Folks' eyes bucked. So...she *did* find it seductive. He really didn't mean for it to be, but he guessed now that it couldn't be avoided.
He knew that the man of God had to be ready for any situation, or emergency that could arise at any given moment. But this one caught him completely off guard. He felt a little surprised that his wife was being so bold. It kind of excited him. He watched her sway her body towards the lounge.
He was in, and back out of the bathroom in two minutes flat.

Pastor Folks still was not sure about when to stop intimate relationships with his wife. So he approached his wife moving very slowly. Donna looked at the expression on his face. She could see the question of caution in it.

"What's wrong?" she asked.

"Are you sure it's...it's, okay, you know? Are you sure it's okay to be intimate at this time?"

Donna had to smile and she released a tiny giggle. But, she wasn't really laughing at him. She knew he meant at this stage of her pregnancy. He was so sweet. He was so protective.

"Is that what's bothering you?"

Looking at her on the Chaise, and wanting her more than ever, all he could do was nod his head.

"Well Quincy Folks. I know you wear many hats."

Donna held up her hand, and began to count off on her fingers.

"You are a son, a brother, a pastor, and (her voice weakened when she looked at his masculine chiseled physique), and need I say, you are a man."

She wanted to say *husband,* but she got side tracked viewing his body.

"Which hat do you want to wear tonight?"

He had to laugh as her reassuring eyes met his. That was all he needed to know.

Lucy Heath

"*First Lady Folks,* you **do** have a way with words."

Quincy lowered himself onto the Chaise, and he forgot about *every* other hat he wore.

TWENTY NINE

The Christmas of 1964 will forever be dear to my heart. For one thing, it reminds me that miracles do happen. Miracles happen all the time, but somehow a Christmas miracle reminds you of Who is in charge. I know even the more that God's protection is His grace and mercy covering us.

Since we had decided to go back to the house on Christmas Eve, and leave out early the next morning, we woke up to an early morning snow. It was forecasted to be a light dusting, but had already accumulated to about three or four inches. I believe by leaving when we did, we may have beaten some of the salt trucks and snow plows to the main roads. If it were the spring of the year, or the summer months, we might have traveled on some of the back roads, but we needed to use the Interstate.

Besides, we already shorted ourselves out of one night stay (*though most enjoyable*), and the more time we spent with Mother Folks in Wilmington, the better.

I believe we both were feeling a little romantic from last night's intimacy. It's kind of funny what this man of God stirs in me. Right now I feel like a shy teenager sitting next to him. At other times I feel boldness in the romance department, and take the lead.

Almost as if he read my mind, Quincy reached over and took my left hand in his. He raised it to his lips, and gave it a tender kiss. The touch of his lips warmed me to my boots. An unexpected gasp escaped my lips, and he crooked his face towards me while still keeping his eyes on the road.

His eyes met mine with a slight flash. I could feel his love and devotion toward me. I knew last night crept into his thoughts too. I knew he was kidding, but he said it anyway.

"Don't make me have to pull this car over."

"You better keep your eyes on the road and leave the *'love making'* to us big girls."

Quincy started chuckling, remembering how in the heat of their passion last night he alluded to ...relishing being loved by a *full grown* woman!

"Oh. No! You didn't go *there*", he said.

"Oh yes I did, and we're going to your mother's house, so get your sanctified mind off *that* until we get back home."

⸻

We took RT340 through Bird-in-Hand, and Intercourse, Pa. We exited onto RT30 W to 'Gap', Pa. because it was a more direct route into Wilmington.

The roads had not been plowed, but because of traffic they were passible. It was still early, about 7:30a and we had another half hour or so to go. I found a radio station that was playing Christmas music. Some songs reflected the excitement and expectations of the season, while others drew your attention to the sacred meaning of the holiday.

Some of the words in one of the songs reminded me that we left before having our morning devotions. I mentioned it to Quincy, and he began to pray asking God to search our souls, and to cleanse and forgive us from all unrighteousness. He prayed for all those who were members of the body of Christ, and for the ones yet to come. He asked for the Lord's blessing on the sheep he was given to shepherd. Then he prayed against any evil assignment or yoke of bondage that the adversary would send upon us; that it be destroyed in the mighty Name of Jesus!

He ended the prayer asking the Father to allow His guarding angels to encamp around us, and to lose them to protect all those traveling on the highways in the Name of the Father, the Son, and the Holy Ghost. Amen.

God's timing is perfect! Quincy no sooner got the prayer out of his mouth when a car came up behind us. It jumped onto the shoulder of the road, and swung in front of us passing us on the right. Before we had time to think, the driver lost control of his car and began to skid from side to side. He must have been trying to steady the car, but it was no use. We could tell the driver was tapping his breaks trying to stop the car. It swerved even more. Maybe what he tried to do after that was to turn the wheel slightly so the car would go into the left lane, evidently he over corrected his turn. The car did a 180° turn and was headed straight for us.

Simultaneously the Name of *'Jesus'* flew out of our mouths. I felt our car slide. Quincy reached his hand across to where I was sitting. I could feel the strength of his hand on my chest trying to hold me against the seat.

He was trying to steer with one hand, hold me with the other, and tap his brakes all at the same time. I could feel the centrifugal force moving my body forward.

After that, everything seemed to be moving in slow motion. I thought I heard his voice. It was saying something...giving some kind of instruction. It sounded very deep, bass-like, and reverberating in my ears. He must have been telling me what he was doing so I wouldn't be afraid.

I could hear it echoing in slow motion.

"Steer...steer, the car...the car...car...slowly...onto... onto...the ...s-h-o-u-l-d-e-r."

After what seemed like an eternity, but clearly must have been only a few short seconds, the car came to a stop on the shoulder of the highway. I was petrified.

I heard a voice talking to me. It seemed to be coming from a distance, but it wasn't. It was Quincy. He was asking me if I was okay. I nodded my head, but he grabbed my face in his hands, and turned it to face him. He wanted to be sure I knew what I was saying.

"Honey, are you okay? Are you hurt? Do you feel like the baby has been injured in any way?

I shook my head to clear it.

"No. No. I'm fine, I'm okay. What about you? Are you alright?"

"Sure, sure, I'm okay. If you're alright, I'm going to check on the other driver."

⁓

Quincy turned the ignition off, and opened the car door. He checked for traffic, and then stepped out on the side of the road. I turned to look out of the back window. I couldn't see much. From what I did see, it didn't look as if any other cars were involved. The driver who pulled in front of us was now sitting in the middle of the median. A few cars and a truck were pulled off to the side, but that was probably just to see what had happened. Other than that, everything appeared to be okay.

After a couple of minutes Quincy came back to the car. He said the young guy in the car kept apologizing over and over again. He was pretty shaken up.

He admitted to Quincy he didn't know what was in store for him when he saw Quincy get out of his car and head towards him. He only knew that whatever was going to happen to him, he deserved it, because he could have killed someone and that included himself as well. He kept saying how stupid and immature he was.

The last thing he expected was for someone to pray for him. Quincy said he had to pray for him in order to calm him down. He was a nervous wreck. The boy thought by now one of the passing cars would have stopped somewhere to call the police. If they had, he just knew he was going to jail.

Quincy said he told the young man that everyone deserves a second chance. This was his! It was Christmas morning, and they were on the highway. Where was someone going to find a Cop? He witnessed to the young man about the goodness of the Lord, telling him that this is why we celebrate this day. It's because of Jesus' birth and death that we all get second and third chances in life. They exchanged contact information, and Quincy said he told him he would be sure to give him a call before the year was out.

⸺

Pastor Folks and Donna held hands thanking God for the miracle He performed in their lives that day. Quincy collected himself, and pulled the vehicle away from the shoulder of the road. He cautiously maneuvered his way back into traffic.

Donna rehearsed the incident over and over in her mind. She asked her husband how he was able to steer the car over to the guardrail, continue to hold her against the seat with the force that he did, and pump the brakes and still avoid colliding with the other car.

Quincy said he had no idea. It was as if everything was moving in slow motion, as if time stood still. He said it wasn't him, it had to be God. Then what he said next caused the hair on his wife's arms to stand up.

"Honey to tell you the truth, I'm not sure what *all* happened. I do know that I couldn't hold you back any longer and maneuver the car too, so when the car was headed for us, I said in my mind: 'Help me Jesus'. Then from out of the blue an auditable voice came to me, telling me to let up off the brakes, and slowly steer the wheel to the right towards the shoulder of the road. I don't even remember turning the steering wheel. All I knew was that I heard a voice, and I was following its instructions."

"Even then", he said:

"It seemed as if the car was lifted up out of the way of the oncoming vehicle."

The rest of the ride to Wilmington was in silence; except for the radio giving praise for the season.

THIRTY

They arrived safely at the house. Pastor Folks asked his mother to have a seat while they shared with her what just happened to them on the Interstate. When she heard their testimony, she knew it was the Lord. She hugged and kissed the both of them two or three times each. She was grateful for the miracle of answered prayers; not just theirs, but hers too. She knew the Lord had prompted her to send up an extra prayer this morning. She thought it was just because of the day, and what it meant to Christians. Now, she sees it was also for the protection of her children.

She was so happy. She cried and clapped her hands praising God for the wonder of His Name!

Donna was alright physically, but a little drained mentally. She excused herself from the excitement to take a short rest. Quincy was on guard, but she assured him she was fine in her body, she just needed to sit for a while in quietness to meditate on the Lord.

The rest of Quincy's family was not going to join them until dinner time, around 3:00p.

As usual the house was decorated beautifully. Before going upstairs Donna toured every room on the first floor. She admired the meticulous attention given to each individual area. Nothing was overdone, or gaudy looking. One could feel the *light*, the *life*, and the *love* of the Savior all around them. It was like each room had a message of its own, and if you stood for a moment in the midst of it, you could hear its words.

Donna moseyed up the stairs and left Quincy and his mother sitting at the kitchen table talking. Although they kept in touch on a regular basis, there was always chit-chat to catch up on. Donna knew how much Quincy loved, and enjoyed his mother's company. They would most likely be down there talking about the baby, what's going on with the church, and sharing the goodness of the Lord with each other.

Donna went to the guest bedroom that she and Quincy shared when they came for recent visits. Her thoughts went back to just one year ago when she had her first overnight stay as *the pastor's lady friend*. She could smile about it now, but she was blushing then when his mother suggested she could lock the door if she was afraid that as a single woman the pastor might tiptoe to her room in the middle of the night. Quincy had the room down the hall that used to belong to his brother. She found out than how jovial his mother could be.

Wow; she thought. *It's only been one year since then.*

Donna walked across the room and sat on the bed. Pleasant thoughts from last Christmas surfaced to her mind.
 'It was Christmas night, and she and Pastor Folks were alone in his Mother's living room. He surprised her with a proposal of marriage, and she said "yes".
 They got married two months later on Valentine's Day.
 'It was then I became 'First Lady' of Lighthouse Christian Ministries. Now, we're expecting a baby this coming May.
 Where did the time go?

Donna moved from the bed to sit at the little writing desk in the corner of the room. Ever since the near accident this morning, words kept floating around in her head. From past experiences when things like that happened she knew to write them down in a journal. She also felt because some of the words were coming to her in verse and rhyme, maybe some sort of poem was being birthed. She often wrote poetry. She wrote the speeches for the Children's programs at church. It's not that they were works to be published; it was something she had a knack for, and something she enjoyed doing.

Donna opened the desk drawer and took out a couple of sheets of the writing paper that belonged to her mother-in-law. A holiday coffee mug sat on the end of the small desk. It held pencils and pens. Donna selected a pencil, not knowing what she'd have to erase if thing didn't flow right. After the first two or three lines she knew it was a poem; not only that, but a title popped in her head: *"The Changing Of the Guards!"*

She knew immediately the poem was going to be about God's angels, and sensed that the poem was prompted by what happened, or *almost happened* to her and Quincy this morning. She breezed through the wording. Some of the timing of the stanzas had to be reconstructed, but all in all, the words flowed, and she wrote them down.

This clearly was no children's poem. No wonder she felt she had to withdraw from the family for a moment. The Spirit Himself placed this in her heart and in her mind, and she had to get it out.

⸺

When Donna entered the kitchen her husband was sitting at the table, and her mother-in-law was standing near the stove. Quincy commented that she didn't rest very long,

Pastor Q and Donna

and could take more time if she needed to. He said they had everything under control for dinner. Donna told them she hadn't rested at all, she's been busy. Pastor Quincy arched his eyebrow in a questioning probe. She lifted the paper in the air, and declared that she spent the time composing a poem, and she believed it was a visionary picture of what 'Guardian angels do when they protect us. Mother Folks wiped her hands on a kitchen towel, and then set the timer in order to track the progress of the sour cream pound cake in the oven. Quincy covered the baking dish that held his famous chestnut cornbread stuffing, and put it on the back of the counter. It was next in the oven after the cake came out.

Pastor Folks suggested they all sit in the living room while Donna read the poem. He went over to the Hi-Fi stereo and turned down the volume on the Christmas album that was playing. Donna was a little nervous. She drew in a deep breath, and said,

"Well here goes." The name of the poem is the changing of the guards."

THE CHANGING OF THE GUARD
As we ring out the old year
And peal in the new
We set goals and resolutions
To change a thing or two

To change what we have been
To take a brand new stand
But there is another changing
That cannot be seen by man

Lucy Heath

I saw a row of angels, standing in the night
But as I approached, to get a closer look
I saw their garments were not so white

Some wings were smoked and tattered
Some arms and limbs were bruised
Some wore bandages on their heads
And others—casts for shoes

Some were slumped and weary-worn
And others did not stand tall
Yet all that stood against that gatepost
Were guarding the "New Year Wall"

In the distance I saw fresh angels descend
And as they entered in the yard
I realized I had witnessed
THE CHANGING OF THE GUARD!

The fresh line came in and took their place
Bid farewell to the old—
It was hard for most to raise their wings
As to the heavens they took hold

These are the ones who protect us
Our dangers they retard
Yes. One night, the Master opened heaven
And I saw the Changing of the Guard.

Pastor Q and Donna

Donna looked up from reading the poem to find both her husband and his mother seemingly in awe. There was a *reverent hush* about the room, and all one could hear was the ticking of the grandfather clock, echoing its heartbeat of praise.

Neither Quincy, nor Mother Folks realized they were holding their breath, until they exhaled at nearly the same moment.

"My, my, my, my, my", was all that Mother Folks could manage to say.

She raised one hand to her face, and covered her mouth. All she could do was to shake her head back and forth. Quincy managed to stand to his feet. He stood placing both hands on his hips. He too, was shaking his head back and forth.

"Well", Donna asked?

Quincy rubbed one hand over the top of his head, as if brushing his hair back. He slowly walked towards his wife.

"I don't what to say. That was the greatest thing I have ever heard. I mean I could almost see what was happening."

"It was beautiful, just beautiful", his mother said.

"I just had to get it down while it was fresh on my mind."

By this time Mother Folks was more composed.

"I always believed that angels exist. I believe they are eternal beings that were created by God to live forever. I even believe in guarding angels. I just never thought that it took any effort on their part to do what they are assigned to do."

"Oh, wait a minute", Donna said. I'm not trying to prove, or disprove anyone's theology on the dispensation of angels. I just wanted to express what I believe came to me (from the Lord) out of my own personal experience."

"Man", Quincy said. "Honey, this poem is really great! I believe the Lord gave it to you, and I believe you were inspired to write it. Don't forget I was there too, and this poem explains some of the things that happened…the things that I can't account for. You know, like the *voice* giving me instructions. And, there is *No* explainable reason **on earth** why our cars should not have collided.

There is no way I could have moved that car fast enough to get out of the way. Not on that ice and snow."

"Yeh, It seems kind of strange…kind of mysterious."

"And, don't forget how you thought I was still holding you back against the seat!"

The kitchen timer went off. Mother Folks rose from her seat to check on the pound cake. Quincy asked to see the poem. He read it through, and shook his head back and forth:

"Um… Um…Um. This is good he said. This is really good, and I'm not just saying that because you're my wife."

⸻

The rest of the family got over to the house around 3:00p. It was a joyous time. We talked and laughed. Of course the brothers brought up a lot of boyhood stories. They had the family really laughing. One of the funniest things about the childhood capers, is that each of them remembered it happening a different way. It took Mother Folks to tell her version of the story to straighten them all out. When she told it the way it really happened; everybody really cracked-up! We snacked on all the goodies that laced the coffee table, end tables, and the side counters and hutches.

We didn't say anything about the baby because Quincy wanted to be the one who told his brother and sister-in-law. I felt good about that, because after all, I was the one who shared it with the parents. We all sat down before dinner to exchange and open our gifts to each other. Quincy was first. He reached under the tree and retrieved the small package I had given to him at our dinner outing. He announced the gift really belonged to both of us, but he wanted to share it with the rest of the family. Quincy shook the rattle like a Christmas bell, and said:

"Merry Christmas to me!"

Then, he held up the little tee shirt that had 'HELLO DADDY' on it in bold letters. His brother jumped up from the sofa, grabbed Quincy with both arms in a bear hug; almost wrestling him to the floor, and kissed him on both cheeks. Then he stood back, shook his brother's hand, and offered his congratulations. They kind of just stood there for a few seconds, and everyone in the room knew it was a *brother moment!* The silence broke, and everybody offered congratulations to the happy couple.

The remainder of the day was great. It wasn't that it was so much about the gifts, as it was about family and fellowship.

Quincy was overwhelmed when he opened his robe. The funny thing about it is that his mother gave him a new bible, and his brother brought him a large cross on a chain. It was the kind pastors wear on the outside of their robes.

I believe before I can get one or two good wears out of the two piece suit he got for me, winter will be over. The blessing is that most husbands aren't sure what size their wives wear. But, Quincy almost got it right. I usually wear a size eight, however in my present condition, I'm sure the size ten he got me will work just fine.

⸻

Mother Folks had some other drop-in visitors. A couple of ladies from her senior group at church, and a few acquaintances who knew that Pastor Quincy was in town came by for a short visit. After the family and other visitors had gone home Quincy could see his mother was weary-worn from the day, but she was happy for it. Still, he encouraged her to turn in for the evening, and we would clear away the food, and clean up the kitchen.

It also had been a long day for the both of us, so we omitted our usual sit on the sofa in front of the fireplace. Quincy turned off the gas logs, and we headed upstairs.

When we got to the top of the stairs, both of us must have been thinking of the same thing...the first Christmas we shared in this house together.

Quincy touched my arm, and when I stopped on the landing. He looped his arms around my shoulders. He drew me close to him, and I caught my breath. His lips brushed mine, and I closed my eyes.

We've had several overnight stays here since our marriage, but standing there in his arms felt like a new beginning in my life.

It could have been the Season.
It could have been the Miracles.
I knew it was the Man!

Epilogue

Just when I needed someone most, the Lord sent my *own* pastor into my life. First he came as a Pastor, then as a friend, and then as a husband. But, to hear Quincy tell it, God sent me into his life.
Who would think that so much could transpire in just a year and a half? Depending on where you are coming from, or where you are on your way to, a short few months can feel like a lifetime. Infatuation is nice, but its *love* that holds everything together.

Quincy clued me in to some of the things I might have to deal with in becoming a pastor's wife, but I know now that you have to allow the Holy Spirit to be you constant companion…your constant help.
Even though I was a newly-wed pastor's wife, I believe Lighthouse Christian Ministries (as small as we were) encountered some of the same experiences that touch some of the larger congregations too. Our experiences may have been on a smaller scale, still we encompassed: weddings, death of a faithful church member, members who chose to leave the church, we dealt with antagonist who chose to stay, and ministered to those who just needed more faith for this Christian walk.

We introduced new training classes for leadership, promoted and extended our outreach program to the needy and to the community, and helped to formulate a united front for clergy in our city. If all of this happened in just one year, it makes me wonder what the future will hold.

Our baby is due in May, so I'll probably work at the hospital through the end of March. I originally thought I would leave in December, but the additional three months will give us the extra income I need to fix up the nursery without bothering the salary the church gives to the pastor. At that time, until we can think of something else, Quincy's study will have to share space with the guest bedroom.
My folks and mother-in-law are spoiling me already. I keep thinking to myself, *'Why am I still working if they are going to buy everything we need for the baby?* But, I really don't mind. They are excited, and they're having fun.

It's a funny thing how I was able to keep my pregnancy a secret for a while, and then it seemed that right after Christmas, I began to expand out of my regular clothes and right into maternity clothes. Luckily, the nurse uniform shops carried maternity ware.

Some of my fondest memories are centered around the sharing and giving of the Christmas season. If I wanted to be spiritual about the doings of God I'd have to say,

"God works in mysterious ways, His wonders to perform."

If I wanted to say it in plain English like the old folks say it, I'd probably say, "God is full of surprises!"

Do you remember Rita? Well some time back she actually repented of the way she was trying to come between the pastor and me. She apologized to me, and *'turned from her wicked ways'*.

She said she had to deal with the truth; that he had chosen me, and not so much that I was looking to marry the pastor. There's nothing wrong with it she said, but she knew she wasn't *'First Lady'* material. She also admitted that when she first signed on to help with the 'Single's Ministry' it was for the advantage of *Rita*. But, after seeing the reaction of the children and the parents at the toy give-a-way, she began to feel differently about it. She jumped into it Gung-ho. Rita also said the real *slap* in the face was when we gave the cross away to Sister Daily. But even when she walked out of service that day, she kept seeing the joy on Sister Daily's face for being appreciated. Rita said she felt that same appreciation when Pastor Folks called her up front, and recognized her as the spearheader of the whole 'Singles' effort, and asked if she would accept the position of being chairperson of the 'Single's Ministry'.

By the way, one of the men she recruited ended up calling her several times, and from what I hear, they're an '*item*'.

I'm glad my appointment to the Pediatrician was at the end of the month. At this time my visits are still once a month. This one particular visit was on the last Thursday in December, the 29th. I felt relieved that my husband could accompany me. It was the last of my vacation, and I had to go back to work in January. I wanted Quincy to be reassured that everything was normal, and I was on track to having a healthy baby.

      I adore living in the spirit of the *season*. The Lord is so generous.

Quincy had that surprise visit from Robert. Actually we both were surprised, but it was on the promise the men made to each other when Quincy visited Robert in the hospital.
I received another surprise for myself and for Quincy too. According to Dr. Cephas, God was not through blessing us with miracles. Another Christmas surprise was in order for the both of us…we were having twins. Wow!

I'm not sure what *'happily ever after'* is, I haven't reached that point yet. I can't even say it's something to be dedicating all of one's efforts to. However, I can say this. Pastor Q and I have had our struggles, and there is no doubt some more may come our way. But for right now, my heart is happy. I look to the future with hope.

Will everyday be filled with perfection?
I expect not. But the lack of a happy moment in my life is just that…a moment. It doesn't negate, or rob me of the joy of my salvation.

"The joy of the Lord is my strength". It is the constant that sees me through hard times. I must trust in the love of the Father, and in the heart of my husband. I love Quincy Folks, and I know without a shadow of a doubt I have been called to walk beside him.

One of the questions we often ask those who come to us for marital counseling is:

> "Is this problem a good thing, or a bad thing?"

> "Is this problem meant to build your marriage up, or to tear it down?"

Of course most agree that the 'bad' things happening in their lives are the negative. Then we share with them what we have to do in our own relationship in times of threat.
It's what Joseph said in forgiveness to his brothers. It's what they also will have to speak to the enemy (the problem) in their times of threat.

> "What you meant (intended) for evil (to harm us) God can turn it to work for our good."

We tell them God intended for the union between Donna and Pastor Folks to be good. We let couples know that God intends the same thing for their marriage too. If they believe it was God in the beginning…then (even through challenges) it will be God in the end!

But we also remind them that the *Word* asked: Is There anything thing too hard for God?

Your love story may not happen at Christmastime, but I pray it will always happen in *God's* time. There is a time give to every season under the heavens. There is a time set for you. There is a season that belongs just to you. So remember: When that season comes into your life, just say…" **yes.**"

To Order: Pastor Q and Donna
www.createspace.com/4731438

Other Romance Novels
By Lucy Heath

Rachel's Forbidden Love
www.createspace.com/3969249

The Reunion
(The sequel to Rachel's Forbidden Love)
www.createspace/4338347

Visit me on:

Amazon Books &Amazon Kindle.com
Facebook: Thewaywewere.LH
http://rachelsforbiddenlove5.webnode.com/
Email: lorene@mail2world.com

Made in the USA
Charleston, SC
12 February 2017